The Ogre of Grand Remous

The Ogre of Grand Remous

Robert Lalonde

Translated from the French by
Leonard   W.   Sugden

Ekstasis Editions

Canadian Cataloguing in Publication Data

Lalonde, Robert
    [Ogre de Grand Remous. English]
    The ogre of Grand Remous

    Translation of: L'ogre de Grand Remous.
    ISBN 0-921215-92-9

    I. Title. II. Title: Ogre de Grand Remous. English.
    PS8573.A38303713   1995   C843'.54   C95-910891-2
    PQ3919.2.L3603713   1995

A translation of **L'Ogre de Grand Remous** *by Robert Lalonde,*
originally published in Paris, France by Editions de Seul, 27, rue Jacob,
Parios VI^(e,) in January, 1992·

Published in 1995 by
Ekstasis Editions Canada Ltd.   **Ekstasis Editions**
Box 8474, Main Postal Outlet   Box 571
Victoria, B.C. V8W 3S1   Banff, Alberta T0L 0C0

The Ogre of Grand Remous has been published with the assistance of a grant from the Canada Council and the Cultural Services Branch of British Columbia.

Printed and bound in Canada by Hignell Printing Ltd.

Tout est employé à boucher le trou par où coule le sang des tiens.
                    Jean Giono, *Deux cavaliers de l'orage*

Tom Thumb, who was very clever, understood his parents' decision and, early in the morning, wanted to go out to search for pebbles.

Charles Perrault, *Tom Thumb*

Thunder rumbles above the cliff. Lower down, the falls are heavily swollen with water (there was so much rain that autumn!) and the dam can scarcely be seen through the blue Chevy's misty windows. The man seated at the wheel is chewing on a cigar and scowling as though he had just been slapped. The woman with the lovely hair goes on talking away without stopping to catch her breath:

"It's tonight or never! Do you understand? I can't take it any more! You've locked me away in that big gloomy house and forced me to make children for you..."

"Forced you?"

"Yes, forced me, forced me!!!"

Her words rise above the storm, above the roar of the dam and the falls. She shouts:

"I want to get away and see the world!"

"We can't do that! The children..."

"You're a weak spineless coward! I should have known. Everything's arranged, you can't back out now?"

"My love..."

"Oh, don't start that! If I were your love, you'd do what I ask. You coward, you coward!"

There's a flash of lightning. The woman screams, climbs out of the car and steps over to the cliff's edge. Beneath the rain and the glimmering sky, she's as splendid as terror itself!

"If you won't come, I'll jump!"

"Wait!"

He too gets out of the car. There's another flash and the woman dangles her left leg in empty space. As he moves towards her, the uproar from the dam muffles the man's voice. But he must have said what she wanted to hear since she reaches out and, in her subdued beauty, allows herself to be led back to the car through the down-pour, her head on his shoulder.

They get back into the Chevrolet and remain there for a while, quietly clutching each other. He weeps as she kisses his wet hair, saying over and over:

"My love, my love, you're splendid!"

A tremendous clap of thunder splits the sky, causing the pines to sway and the dam to quiver. An earth-shaking rumble echoes over and over beyond the cliff top, louder than the roaring water...

Dear Charles,

     I've looked over the first cuts of your *Julien the Magnificent* which has left me puzzled, to say the least. Sure, the frames for this film are quite beautiful. This Grand Remous you've talked so much about appears almost as mythical as in your descriptions and your brother is quite clearly the astonishing character you depicted him to be one evening last year in the studio bar. So, what is it then that really doesn't come off? Well, it's precisely because it sticks too close to what you were trying to do with it! Not a single sequence that doesn't go along, from every angle, with the scenario we discussed together at length, the one that was meant to be a "first draft" and that was to "lead to other things."

     Perhaps it was a mistake to talk to me so much about your rather extraordinary life story. You see, while watching your film, I just couldn't help wanting to know more. Not only about Grand Remous which, may I say again, is merely landscape (very beautiful at that!) in your film—but about Julien himself, about his "madness" and about your past. For example, what was your sister, Aline, "the silent one" like years ago, and what became of her (you told me she wanders about the world, an "eternal fugitive")?, what about your brother, Serge, "the seer," and later, an American gigolo and finally, yourself, for you are nowhere to be found in this film! All your efforts to be objective come more from self-criticism than from professionalism, speaking as one might of our critics who are bound to show themselves much more critical regarding *Julien the Magnificent* than your "demanding but gentle producer" is here.

     I don't wish to keep on. I can only guess what may be the reservations—the fears—that keep you from "plunging blindly into the Messier tragedy" as you so aptly describe it. However, how many "interesting" films will you make before giving us Grand Remous, the WHOLE of Grand Remous, both the chaos and the light in your bewildering family history?

     Do you know, in my wallet I still have that newspaper clipping you'd given me dating back to the spring of 1966. It shows you, your brothers, your sister and yourself, on the steps of that big gray house—"the four orphans of Grand Remous" says the caption —clinging to one another, four little wild animals drawn out of their lair, staring about, with their overly thin arms and tousled hair. And this single phrase, beneath the photograph, which is meant to be eye-catching (pure journalism!). "Their parents are gone forever!"

You've provided me a bit too often with an occasion for not minding my own business, Charles, and I'm not going to let you cover up your Grand Remous now with this *Julien the Magnificent*. These four human destinies that crisscross without ever really making contact...

Look your footage over again and think this over. After the usual bad quarter of an hour (with its feelings of defeat and inertia, when you'll say "I'm a lousy film maker" and perhaps indulge yourself even further along the same lines), you'll come back to an even keel and we'll be able to discuss what to do with this film. But I beg you, Charles, keep in mind, THE film (including its brazen and terrifying elements!) is still to be made and now, more than ever before, I'll be there to help you get it going!

Your producer and "nonetheless friend",

André Lapointe

Julien the Magnificent
(Charles)

André is definitely right, the film's empty. It tells us neither what Julien was nor what was to become of him. I looked the whole thing over, the scenes filmed at Grand Remous and also the "interviews" with him. The sequences on the hill and those shot in the *cabane à sucre* are the best. He doesn't speak, but from his gaze and his gestures: it would be nice to have been mistaken from the very start, he's probably going to crack, to give in and own up to his trickery.

I was as crazy as he was for two weeks. The crew put up with me. They all seemed to sense, to suspect something was going on, that this film was important to me, this autopsy of my brother's illness.

I might have imagined as much. Although his letter in response to my suggestion that we should make this film was warm and "brotherly," there was something frenzied, something of his old ravings about it, rather than the "clinically established over-excitability" we had finally grown used to, Serge, Aline and I. He had written:

You know very well, Charlie, that with us it's things that talk, not people. Whether it be he who stayed or those who are absent. You won't get over it if I were to repeat what Pinceau, our Irish setter, said when he came back all soaking wet from the creek with his mouth bristling with crayfish. Or the daubs of the big heron on our sister, Aline's painting, or that green pigeon forever perched on that funny window way up above the barn, the one called "the Trinité Lauzon grotto" because, you remember, it's up there the giant, Trinité Lauzon, the one who lived in the cabin near the dam, was struck by lightning while pitching hay into our barn. What the water in the creek told me, above all in April when the little spring break up (the big one, of course, is when the ice cracks on the Gatineau river lower down) swept along its winter secrets among the ice and seaweed: the pages of missals tossed into the current after November vespers which you all used to find a punishment, Aline, Serge and yourself (I never went,myself, of course) the fishing rods and rusty stoves of fishermen who had been caught by a sudden freeze up downhill from the dam,

12

and then, the hat ribbons of blossoming young girls surprised by the strong autumn wind as they strolled along. Nor will I repeat to you here the discourse I alone had a right to hear each autumn, lying in the grass on the great meadow, the sermon of frightfully talkative crows, interwoven with dark terrible words: February, March, Lent, illness, death, future, war, father, mother, solitude and company! All these words that fled their ragged wings and came to be caught in my hair like bats, nesting there the whole of November and December until the joyful arrival of Santa Claus' reindeer in the sky over the hill, don't you remember, Charlie?

To answer your long letter with all its twists and turns and, if I've understood you properly: no, I have no objection to you coming to "steal my secrets," as you call it. (Besides, they're yours as well, those secrets that you don't seem to remember.) You'll see, it's the finest time of the year. It's in rather rusty gold and silver and it burns under "a summer sun that wants to spend the winter right here," as Serge used to say at one time. You can film all that quite peacefully and carry on working at it till All Saints without any trouble. Go ahead, but I'm telling you right now that (even if you already know, you once even paid to know!) I don't really fit in too well. I don't know very much about the world you live in or your city ways (you're still on Gaspé Street, I wasn't aware of that!) I haven't set foot in a city for at least seven hundred years, that is to say, since I was in the clinic (may God spare its soul!). All the cells of my memory have been renewed (oh! the doctors would be astonished) and from time to time all I can recall is your half sad, half angry look when we left for Maniwaki. That was the longest trip I ever made! Once in a while on certain evenings, I can still feel myself being borne along between two rows of hazy poplars towards some unknown place where you'd never be able to find me again.

Yes, Charlie, I'm coming back to that again: we used to talk with things and listen to them too, remember! We used to learn a lot! But unlike the three of you, I was never afraid. I was born that way, you know very well: my lonely ways, my head crammed with cockeyed compasses and connected up with invisible, perhaps even dangerous, antennas . . .

I fast-forward the tape on the editing table. Julien is sitting on his swing. He's talking about Aline and that often mentioned time she ran off across the hill. As he tells it, Aline had come back with her body all swollen with bee stings, but with her face shiny and smooth, and she hadn't said a word for three days, because she had seen, because she had finally understood that *there was never any explanation for things nor would there ever be any!* Those stories, our stories, our imaginings, Grand Remous, our prison, the mansion with its four orphans. Then, their absence that we kept on trying to fathom (except for Julien who, in his way, had already fathomed everything), mama and papa's disappearance, their running off in the middle of the night—they had said that they were going fishing at the dam at Baskatong—, skipping out, deserting us. Aline's early morning howls from down in the meadow and Julien's stubborn silence, he who, the evening of that first day, had begun to believe he was born of the Holy Ghost. And then, all the books from their library lying open night and day on the table, in our beds, on the living room floor: where had they gone? What was it existed out there in the world that was so beautiful, more beautiful than their own four children? Geography books, maps, globes: Gaspésie, Maine, Massachusetts? Papa had often spoken of Percé Rock, the lakes at Maskinongé, Maine, Boston where our uncle, Paul Dumouchel, our father's idol, had studied the violin. . . History books: wasn't mama interested in the Civil War, in the poor slaves in the cotton fields? And so, back to the geography books, Richmond, Charlottetown, huge Virginia: it was all so confusing! (The cotton fields, the slaves, the war: of course, in our minds, all these things existed at the same time we did, somewhere south of Grand Remous.) Mama's novels, their pages carefully thumbed through, and then, our memories of their conversations at the swing where they spoke of doing great things, of becoming useful, of counting for something in the world! Not for a second did we believe that they had been in an accident, that they had gotten lost or been kidnapped. They had simply decided to run off and see the world!

They had loved us and given us everything. We were now grown children (except for Julien!), and there was the fertile earth, the

14

machinery and the river: Grand Remous was ours. As for our parents, the world still expected ... great things! And then, we had this money at the *Caisse populaire*: the often proclaimed twenty-six thousand dollars! They had never mentioned leaving and, at the same time, had never really talked about anything else: it was always Virginia, Gibraltar, Tierra del Fuego. We knew they had left never to return. For the first twenty days Aline kept howling and weeping. There was only Julien, the youngest, who didn't seem to be aware, who never would be. Who the devil was it the three of us kept on talking about? Mama? Papa? Who were they? The house, the hill, the creek, the river, the four of us and... the voices were the only things that really existed.

For Julien who was devoid of suffering, who was in paradise, who never looked into himself, who would never leave Grand Remous where he was miraculously born, where he was perhaps alone and unbalanced but never abandoned, the world spoke to him and silently revealed its mysteries. Ourselves, we were impenetrable, argumentative and unhappy. We didn't go mad. We went away. We left the river, the house and the hill. We deserted paradise: it's we who got lost.

Slithering up to the top of the oak tree with my thighs wrapped around its bough's skin-like smoothness. I raise the machete to hack off a branch that had been struck by lightning. For a moment I lose my breath. Oh, it doesn't last very long! Immediately, dusk is upon me. The tree's cool flesh is under my belly. I had just thought: "I've too much blood in my body, too many heady odours in my nostrils, my mouth runs with too many tastes and tangs." And I found most troublesome this over-abundance, my body's loneliness, the summer fading and the slightly sickening delicacy of sundown. Then the machete whistled through the air as I gave a fierce swing. Was it this movement, my breath rasping like a fettered animal's, that did it? I thought I saw legs, pale arms and, fleeing through the reeds, a lovely face under a tangle of dark hair. With one blow, I expel the foul air from my lungs, close my eyes and wait. My mind a pale void, I grow dizzy. I open my eyelids and perceive nothing but the daylight flitting through the pines. A hairy woodpecker darts across a corner of the sky above me.

The flame of the setting sun knifes through the crest of pines. The river mirrors the row of black trees. Perhaps, over there, there's a figure crouching in the ferns. If I see that apparition again, later, in the light of day, I shall gallop and howl down the foot trails. . .

"Gone to Europe? France? Paris?"

"But where would they get the money, since they left all of their savings with us?"

"You don't believe it was all they had!"

"Maybe they took a plane? or maybe a boat?"

"Maybe they sold the house and someone will soon come along with a truck to take it over and make us leave!"

It was Aline who expressed this fear. The house wouldn't be taken, we were soon to learn. Serge and I endeavoured to console Aline but she wouldn't listen. We kept on repeating that they hadn't done it with us in mind or, to be more precise, hadn't done it against us. We'd get along. We had the farm to fall back on. And then, we wouldn't have to go to school any more! Even you, Aline, got bored with it. Poor Miss Talbot couldn't teach you anything—you knew more than she did and that humiliated her; as a result, you stayed away every other day. You used to go off in the fields collecting plants with Serge and Mama, searching for *epifagus virginiam* or *ambrosia trifida*. Julien only attended school for a month. He told the teacher about his dreams, made his comrades laugh with his stories and our stories. He didn't learn a thing nor did he want to. Anyway, like the rest of us, his knowledge was innate. Papa kept on telling us over and over: "Knowledge is inborn! Everything was already within you at birth! Let them go on moralizing and prattling away, your teacher, the curé, the bishop, the pope and the prime minister, all these ignorant types that get carried away!" and he would laugh so loud the windows would shake. So Julien didn't go back to school. Papa let him live like a *coureur de bois*, a Robinson Crusoe, Davy Crocket. "He's discovering the forest, the animals and the world all around, and that's just fine! Later on, he'll find out about ... the rest. That can wait!", he used to say mysteriously. Our little brother had plenty of time whereas we, the older ones, we had to be sensible. In any case, we had already begun going out a great deal. "All you need is courage, just a bit of courage, the rest of you! And things won't be so difficult. As for Julien, that's something else!" What was it, then? Why didn't Julien need courage? Because he was weird, mad?

17

Probably, Papa was trying to protect him, to prevent him from being hurt. Aline kept on and on with her questioning:

"But, Papa, what good will maths, geometry and catechism be to us?"

Georges would sigh, raise his hands with palms upward as a wide gesture of a Mister Know-it-all who's not going to waste his time with "naïve dunderheads":

"Courage, Aline! Courage, my daughter!"

What we needed was courage. For Julien, it was stories, Daniel Boone and rafts he would build to float down the creek on Easter mornings while we, Aline, Serge and myself, went off to church. Because, after all, that was where we, the rest of us, had to go in search of courage in our Sunday outfits that we had to iron ourselves, because Mama was reading *Gone with the Wind* in her canopy bed made of mosquito netting that had been found in the barn, the one with that funny skylight, "the giant Trinité Lauzon's grotto."

You're not aware, Julien, that I looked for them all over the world, that I still am searching and so is Aline; however, we have lost that courage Papa used to speak of and that we learned about at church and at school: courage through faith and courage through love. I didn't go crazy, myself. Nothing was ever told me by a psychiatrist or by voices. I make films out of other peoples' stories and from yours too, Julien, and this one's a failure. I should. . . I should have. . . But no, whether it be the films or, just as long before, our great crusades in search of our parents, the doctors, forgetfulness: nothing will ever wipe all of this away, the four of us, the past, their desertion and you, Julien, whom we lost.

I start the camera again. It's that muddy cascading creek. We're all standing above the great meadow. The sun, along with the water flowing down the stream, makes glistening gold, jade and bronze. I shouted to the cameraman who wanted to know what we were to take next:

"Keep taking the flowing water!"

And he obeyed. Ten minutes of this splashing frothy current, it was all so far away now! It came to me: "When I look all of this over, something will come back to me. For the moment, I can neither see nor imagine anything. Maybe I'll add Julien's voice to these pictures. He'll talk about our past get-togethers fishing, grey trout in the spawning season, Serge's swimming prowess and then, maybe I'll hear and I'll see something. I'll finally come to understand that the

18

world isn't closed off for me forever; finally, I'll sense something! "I made this film for myself, Julien, not for you. And it's a waste of effort. I'm here gazing at it and knowing that never will any light be shed on our story. Nothing has ever changed and the past is catching up with me and you are too, Julien. Often, while staring at the picture of the waterfall, my gaze grows hazy and I can perceive Serge splashing about in the creek; he's like a real fish swimming with the current and mama bends over him, kisses him, strokes his soaking wet head that has just emerged from the water like a trout, and is about to dive again just as fast.

"My love, my love, you're a champion!"

She had said that all in one breath, like some enraptured actress, her eyes opened wide, her hand holding her straw hat with its blue ribbon fluttering in the wind. Serge was off with the current, dashing along like an eel through the rapids, and we would follow him, mama and I, running along the river bank. Mama would raise her head and look at me now and then. Yet, I could scarcely see her face in the hat's dappled shade and I knew, *I knew* I shouldn't look at her and that I would never ever be able either to forget or to remember her really.

Even before her disappearance, mama was never anything but an image. I never had anything else but that, images. I only receive images, Julien, like you only have voices. Are Aline and Serge really alive? They probably aren't either. Aline has her travels and her roaming about, and Serge his loves and his false *dolce vita*. Serge is borne away by the current, Aline flies in the wind, I am held back by the force of the earth and Julien is burnt by fire. And it is forever the water from the creek, the breeze from the hill and the pine forest set ablaze by ancient suns. It will forever be Grand Remous, an impossible love, an impossible oneness and an impossible forgetting.

19

Certainly we waited for them. We knew they wouldn't return but we waited. One evening or one morning, they would be there with their dusty clothes, their eyes darting out of their heads with fatigue and anguish, somewhat older, and perhaps scarcely recognizable, but back with us again. We were haunted by their remoteness and how they had slipped away. We used to imagine them off there so far away, alone and trembling, so lonely and not knowing what to do with the tender feelings they always had for us and that now seemed so pointless. Smothered ourselves by those same feelings, we imagined them exhausted and at their wits' end with guilt and remorse. Mama would be emaciated and speechless, with her hair ruffled and her dress torn, spreading her arms and throwing back her head like a tall little child gone partly mad. She was the orphan girl and we were the wasteful parents. Then, there was Papa; his head would be shaven, his old wool jacket at one time stained with ink but now stained with blood, his great knotty hands dangling loose and trembling before him, his awkward smile, his vacant gaze saying: "There's nothing at all out there in the world, nothing at all. It's all here with you. . ."

We always limited our imaginings, never really evoking the hugs and tears we'd shared. Scenes of our reunion grew hazy and improbable. Aline couldn't weep any more and her voice had cracked. Serge was drained of his strength. He had already demolished papa's workshop, torn apart his butterfly collection, thrown his pipes and cigar boxes out across the field and burned all his copies of the *National Geographic*. Myself, I had relieved my distress with arguments and explanations, theorizing about dates and itineraries, meridians and latitudes, their stop-overs, points where they might turn back and the traces left along unknown routes. As for Julien, we often went searching for him. He used to run off. With our big flashlight we would organize "beats" throughout the countryside, often until dawn. For me, he was playing games; it wasn't possible he didn't remember; maybe he was furious over their disappearance and would kill himself, leap into a ravine or slip his head into a wolf trap. Some demon had hold of him. Julien didn't know himself what had gotten into him when he'd run off deep into the forest for three days at a time without a thing to eat. On each occasion, we'd come back from our hunting totally stymied. Then, just when we thought he was either dead or had run away, Julien would suddenly appear, smiling with mama's eyes, carrying a hare in each hand dripping with blood. Aline would strike him, hurl herself at him with all her remaining strength. Then, Serge would catch hold of Aline and pin her down on the living room couch. I'd go to Julien and try to talk to him once more :

"Don't you realize? They've gone! Forever!"

"Who's that?"

He looked at all three of us like a sleepwalker, dragging his muddy boots into the kitchen where he skinned and cut up the hares, drenching the table and counters with dark blood.

Then, in the morning, a man and woman came from Maniwaki. It's Serge who spotted them first from our bedroom window.

"Oh! oh! This is the beginning of the end!"

We went down to receive them in the kitchen. Thunder was rumbling above the hills; it had been so hot for several days. We had been waiting for a storm for a week. We hadn't slept very much; Julien hadn't come home. Aline made some coffee. She had dug out one of mama's pretty dresses from the attic and tied up her hair. You could have taken her for seventeen! (She was fifteen, I sixteen, Serge fourteen and Julien was nine).

Serge and I, grave and dignified in our suits and ties, were seated at the end of the table.

Our parents? They had gone to one of our mother's sisters living in Virginia; she was ill. Gone forever? Come now, that's impossible! Who could have told them that, for heaven's sake?

"This is a paltry joke!"

Just by myself, I acted scandalously enough, beating all the hypocrites of Grand Remous by far. Our youngest brother? He was asleep upstairs with a severe case of hay fever. Then came the first crackle of lightning and the woman let out a shriek. Aline served coffee again, but we didn't drink. We had to keep our nerves intact. Serge asked why they had left their car at the bottom of the hill.

"The road is perfectly drivable, you know!"

He was quite splendid and the man was impressed. He would say to his bosses: "They are well behaved, well educated, quite self-reliant and grown up and oh, so very composed! What's being said about that family is nothing but wicked tongues busy with their empty twaddle!" And that would be all. We didn't blush, we didn't even quiver. We kept our hands on our knees, didn't get the pleats in our pants crinkled and maintained an appearance that was serious, polite and as smooth as our shirt collars. With the second flash of lightning followed by an immense not-too-distant clap of thunder, the woman started to shake. Aline's playacting was beginning to fail her. She stood up and offered to show them the library. I quickly broke in:

"Perhaps another time! I think it would be better to get on the road before the storm really gets going!"

I wasn't anxious for them to see the library, the books left lying open all over the place, the maps and globes of the world, imagined itineraries marked out on papa's old newspapers. . .

They left as the rain really came pouring down, taking along mama's umbrella and promising to bring it back on their next visit. They never did come back. I'm not so sure they believed us. We were peculiar, an odd tribe with its own laws and mysteries, an outlandish bunch or whatever you like, but surely not abandoned children. I think we frightened them. And then there were the twenty-six thousand dollars in the bank! There was positively no need to feel sorry for us!

That evening, Aline lost her voice again, but her tears came back, joyful and triumphant tears. We were proud, all three of us, for having foiled them, feeling quite high and mighty about our clever lies and about this storm that had come just in the nick of time, that cleansed us of guilt, so to speak, and brought us rain to make our corn grow, our only food that summer. We were exultant as well because of Julien's absence for he surely would have ruined everything.

However, we were alone, now, once and for all. That evening, you would have thought we wanted to be.

I'm speaking to you without really speaking to you, Charlie, but I know you can hear me. I'm going to talk to all three of you and I know you'll hear me. And I know you'll come back!

You're spying on me, Charlie, as though I were some quarry you were after. You have the look you had ten years ago, with something else that's a bit unhappy or sad behind those glasses. Even your friends don't seem to understand you very well, with their cameras and their wires, city people following us, lost in the high grass on the hillside. I can hear the woodcock squawking with fear over there in the undergrowth and I see you setting up to take your pictures. Your camera and your tape recorder remind me of those doctors' machines that left me completely stupefied. Why, sure, I'm talking quite a bit, just as I did at the clinic. It's just to get on your right side, to make you laugh.

Charlie, the wind's really high and the house is creaking all over. Listen, Charlie, the wind speaks with every gust just like Aline when she's angry and, just as in her case, it doesn't frighten me. Listen to the wind with me, Charlie, and give it up, I beg you! It's the wind that makes you fall silent around the table, when you have traced out route after route on the backs of pages torn from calendars and when you grow silent, Serge, Aline and yourself, when there are no more cries and no more tears. The terror is borne away by the fine wind that engulfs the house and you finally manage to forget without falling asleep. You lean your heads together and, with me, you listen to the wind. Suddenly, we are from nowhere else, we have been here forever, alone with the wind, and you finally understand that we are going nowhere, that we will never go anywhere else. The world is becoming once again round and soft as a peach, like Aline's cheek, like your knee, Charlie, beneath my hand, me, a happy little animal. You've abandoned your cursed mania for origins and tracing people's pasts. Suddenly you're with me, in the same time and the same space as I, as the house, as the wind, as the river we can sense through the living room window, cascading along endlessly. It's miraculous luck, our luck—there's no one present to know, to dictate or to hinder us! At long last, you understand that! I know very well it won't last, that you'll begin again, either during the night or in the morning, trembling and talking away, hunting through books and disappearing from my world. But for an hour, at least, I have friends and

23

accomplices, no longer merely brothers and a sister; three warm tender bodies, three brains unable to fantasize. You are with me, you are mine. I can touch you, caress you, make you laugh and tell you about what the wind sings to me so softly. There is nothing more beautiful than this solitude that gives us everything without asking for something in return. No other time exists outside the eternal present. We are three Adams and an Eve, the first and only ones. There will be no fall, no forbidden tree other than the birch and spruce and, living without masters and gods, we are free to taste any fruit without their permission. Oh! How you laugh! You gasp for breath; you growl, pick me up and catch hold of me again on the living room couch and then, books, maps, the pages of calendars with all their false time and space are crushed beneath me, their crumpling sounds bringing my body relief. No longer do you feel destitute since you are no longer troubled and unhappy. Tomorrow, when it comes over you again, I'll merely have to disappear into the woods. I'll go and listen to the martin and the fox, for as long as you keep going doggedly on. And I'll come back for these get-togethers when your laughter, your hands, your eyes ...

My big brother, you're wasting your time trying to understand. You're better at counting the grains of sand on the beach by the dam. You get angry when, urged by Aline, I come down to bring you a sandwich. I rush up behind you, you jump and forget how many. Eight thousand seven hundred and thirty-seven? Nine thousand eight hundred and thirty-seven? Then you leap on me and, furious and gasping for breath, wrestle with me on the sand; tomorrow, you'll have to start over again! But you simmer down quite quickly and all those grains you have already counted, having now forgotten how many and that you placed one by one in a jam jar, you let them flow between your fingers with the odd smile of a sage or a holy martyr.

In your film, the house will never give up any of its secrets. It will only show off its old charm, that poor old charm capable of stirring the fancy of citizens eager for images of another world. On your tapes, the songs of birds, the soft murmurings of the creek, the creaking of the stairway and the sound of my voice will be captured forever and forever ring as though they were false. As you are quite aware, you can admire a wolf in his pen, but never come close and get to know him, know how he hunts and what makes him howl when the moon is full. Why would others have to understand us, Charlie? Just how would that make us happier or more free? How would that bring them any closer?

The film won't be shown. I know now that I didn't make it for anyone, that I took these shots for the other one, that unknown savage, half Julien and perhaps, half myself, his brother. I am tired; however, I won't sleep. I remain shut away here playing tapes over and over on the machine, the sounds and images, Julien, Julien's voice and from time to time my own, an already aged and often faltering voice that I fail to recognize:" No, no, don't stop! Wait a bit! Keep it going! . . ." It's here and now, this very night, that I let it run and don't cut it off, playing over and over again, of course, the great scene of betrayal.

After his agitated telephone call, I had arrived at Grand Remous at night. I knew it would be frightful: taking Julien away, simply getting him out of the house would be like attempting to lift a wild or injured dog into a car to get him to the vet's. If I didn't play my cards right, he'd know; he'd catch on, disappear into the woods and I'd never have the courage to try it again. I had rolled, as the song goes, "between two greyish green walls of spruce," expounding all kinds of increasingly more fanciful schemes. Later, much later, I was to see how thoughtless, frightened and cowardly I was. But that night, I did my duty. Yes, I lied to him, but it was for his own good! To take care of an enraged animal accustomed to hurling itself against the bars of its pen you don't ask for its cooperation! He had repeated attacks. He was frightened himself by the last one; I had found him down by the creek with his forehead all bloody and his body as limp as an old rag. He was frothing at the mouth and gasping like a fish out of water. I carried him on my back up to the house and to his room where I bandaged him and put him to bed. Then I got hold of Aline on the phone.

"Are you sure, Charlie, are you sure of what you're saying?'
"Positively!"
"Oh, my God! . . ."

And once again I repeated it: in Julien, they lived together, just as do day and night, the immortal and guiltless child, born of the gods and free as the winds, and the monster, the wolf who was responsible for our family's becoming unhinged. Aline was choking with tears on the phone.

"This is senseless, Charlie, senseless!. . ."
"Aline, trust me and do as I ask!"

25

"I suppose there's no other choice, now. But Oh my Lord! He's going to kill himself!"

"No, he won't. Everything's going to be all right!"

We held on without saying a word for a good long minute filled with darkness and the distant hum of other voices on the line. Then Aline said: "Okay!" and she hung up. Reason was on our side, poor us. Then, there was this miracle. The next day, Julien climbed into the car beside me without asking any questions, sitting there, his head wrapped in a bandage, his eyes expressionless, his great heavy arms lying motionless on his lap. When we reached the highway, he simply asked in a dull voice:

"Where are we off to, Charlie?"

I didn't answer. I'm sure he'd caught on and that he merely wanted to hear me say those words: *clinic, doctor, examinations*. He wanted to hear aloud from me the ugly phrase that would put a finishing touch to this betrayal, this plot against him. Aline was waiting for us at the Maniwaki clinic in her old red woolen overcoat, pale, her hair a mess, her shoulders hunched. He smiled at her when he saw her and Aline took his arm. We entered the clinic as solemn and silent as you would a church. The formalities (Oh! father's first name, mother's family name, feverishly whispered by Aline into the nurse's ear!), the room number and then, the elevator. Once in the room, he immediately buried himself under the sheets, refusing to put on the white shirt the nurse had left discreetly on the bed. Only his left foot stuck out from the shapeless hump formed by the sheets. Then, he yelled:

"Now, get out! Get out!"

Aline was crying, of course. She wept until we got to Montreal, until I turned off the motor in front of her place. We had to talk about it a bit just the same. I told her it was all for the best. She said that she still had hope but that it was as though she were dead and that it was "all THEIR fault." I kissed her. The car windows got all foggy. There was a long silence between us, then she opened the door and ran up the stairs to her apartment. I drove home where Serge was waiting for me. He was drunk and kept saying over and over:

"You're a genius, Charlie! Myself, I wouldn't have been able. . . I couldn't have done it! "

We had handed you over to the doctors, Julien. That night, there was no way we could have forgiven ourselves, not so very soon. But what else were we to do?

26

Her name's Irene; she told me so. She's living in the ogre Trinité's former hideaway. I followed her, this evening, as far as the shack close by the dam. She rebuilt the old shack herself. She says: "Now, it's my cottage," and invites me in. Who would have thought that one day, my brothers, I would go near the ogre Trinité's cabin without falling dead on the spot ?

She doesn't understand, of course, why my limbs are trembling as I sit beside her on the cabin's steps. I can't tell her. I can't yet, Irene! I repeat her name, as I cool down: "Irene, Irene, the Sleeping Beauty ..." She laughs and asks: "Why the Sleeping Beauty?"

I'll tell her. Yes, I'll tell her everything, bit by bit.

He had piled the books, maps and photos in the bedroom. Our former bedroom, where I used to go and sleep after a day of filming, had become the orphans' museum. Julien's now sleeping in the attic in the old brass bed surrounded by all Aline's early sculptures, her fat clay suns painted yellow and black. The crew slept downstairs on folding cots. Of course, on the first evening I choked on dust opening books and spreading out maps. Seated on my old bed, I went sorrowfully back over all our once imagined itineraries by lamplight and found these old hypothetical paths more real and more promising than the many trips I would make years later when still on their trail.

In a school scribbler with a collie dog on the cover, Aline had glued some photos of Virginia she had cut from the *National Geographic*. A tobacco field at sunrise, three black working men ("They're slaves!") leaning against a high wooden fence in one of Atlanta's lower quarters, a trawler filled with cotton, like some allegorical chariot, in the port of Savannah. The captions under these photos spoke of a country that was magnificent although ruined and sad. In the middle of the scribbler, the famous photograph of a flaming sunset with Clark Gable and Virginia Leigh, their dark silhouettes cut out from the dust jacket on Carmen's *Gone with the Wind*. Aline had recopied certain passages from the novel underlined by our mother and likely to put us on some trail or other. Ten years later, I got off the train at Atlanta. I made a tour of the hotels and motels with their photos. There was no more wooden fence or black workers in overalls smiling sadly, and above all, there wasn't, nor had there actually ever been a Carmen and Georges Messier in that unrecognizable hectic up-to-date city.

Our globe of the world still lit up. So I started a game we had once played. I closed my eyes, spun the earth and let my finger drag along the cold sphere until it stopped. When I opened my eyes again, my finger was pointing at the Bismarck Archipelago, north of New Guinea. Why not? Maybe that's where they were, in a bamboo cabin by the seashore, warming their old bones in the sun. The earth was so big.

I stretched out on the bed, not thinking of anything. Sliding my hand under the pillow, I touched the smooth cold cover of a thick book: Perreault's *Tales*! The pages were warped; some were smeared with Aline's saffron yellow. In the margins, drawings, some kind of cabalistic signs, arrows, a phrase from Tom Thumb underlined here and there: "Tom Thumb heard everything they said. . .", "The father and mother, seeing they were busy working, stole away . . ."

Suddenly the door began opening slowly. Julien was there on the threshold, pale, naked, with his mouth open and a blank stare in his eyes. I rose. He kept shaking his head as though to say no. I approached him. He was trembling. When I touched his shoulders, he uttered a small cry like a trapped animal, then slipped to the floor like a puppet that had become unstrung. I picked him up and lay him on Serge's bed. His breathing was steady and he was asleep: the crisis had passed. Not too serious a case of sleep-walking and a slight aberration; it was a false alarm.

When I woke up, Julien was no longer on the bed where the pillow and eiderdown had been carefully straightened. I could hear him laughing with the crew downstairs and the odour of his ham omelet filled the whole house.

I shouldn't start at it again, otherwise he would start again too.

The pine forest had taken her in so quickly! Before there was an ogre and now it's the Sleeping Beauty. Between the branches, the light patches of her skin, the dark wet shimmer of her hair! Her fragrance blends in with the pine balm and the sharp fiery song of the cicada greets her; copying my earlier voice, the hissing of a thirsty snake.

Like me, she has no origin. We speak a lot through gestures. She appears and disappears, like the ghosts used to in that white hospital. But she is quite real, knowing how to make fire, how to touch and laugh, how to open and close those eyes which are sometimes pale fires, sometimes sparks that ignite the whole of me. She walks to the edge of the sluice gate, waves her hand above her head and calls to me gently. She says she recognized me and that, at the same time, I am a stranger. I knew myself that the long hundred year sleep was coming to a close.

Now we roam about Grand Remous, the tiny beach, the hillside and the pinewood together. I still can't go into the cabin. "Later, I told her, when I'll have gotten over him." She said: "Gotten over whom?" "The ogre," I answered. She laughed and said: "I have to get over my ogre too!" Then, I learn there was a man in town who had frightened her. I told her: "I know what fear is, myself, and I'm no longer afraid of it." She laughed, showing all her teeth, and I placed my large free hand on her arm. She too has to get back at life. We shall help each other and all will be well.

I stop at a certain frame: Julien trembling a little, his inexplicable expression. His deep set eyes with their slightly greenish glimmer. His prominent cheekbones still dotted with bristles from a poor shaving job, a long mop of reddish blond hair covering his brow. And that enigmatic smile!

At an early age, he never let himself be photographed. In the album, he is always seen either turned away or making faces. When Aline would take this album on her knee, which to us was a sort of Bible, Julien would grow edgy, bring up the raspberry bushes that needed pruning, and finally rush out slamming the door. All of these portraits, these rigid landscapes, this past that we kept on scrutinizing passionately, only served to deprive him of his confidence, of his faith in us now, in this eternal present that he wanted for us all.

One evening, we even forced him to look at it. Serge held him down on the bed (in a Chinese wrestling hold) and Aline turned the pages while I shouted above his howls: "This is your papa, Georges, and you're riding on his shoulders! And that, that's her, Carmen, our mother! Look, you've got her eyes!" But he wouldn't look, despite Serge's fingers pulling at his eyelids.

The next morning, all three of us examined the tiny mauve marks he had around his eyes, traces of our futile violence and of his stubbornness in believing he had grown like an onion, had been found under a cabbage leaf or had fallen into our garden in a hailstorm. And we all went off laughing idiotically when he applied two drops of butter to his eyelids, saying that he had burned himself again with the blow torch while repairing the threshing machine.

Early in the morning, we went down to the little beach. Our feet left small bird-like prints in the sand. Aline and I carried the books and maps, Serge, the fruit, the fishing rod and the net. The adventure was under way, a picnic at Veracruz or in the West Indies. We gave ourselves completely over to this game, improving our knowledge, unconsciously preparing ourselves to leave as well. The keys on the maps became a key to them, and then, quietly, our own. The highest point above sea level: Mount Everest, 29,028 feet; the highest active volcano: Cotopaxi, Equador, 19,347 feet; the deepest lake: Lake Baikal, 5,714 feet; the largest island: Greenland,842,800 square miles. Each of us gave the class, each in turn asking questions, then answering. Aline bit into an apple and roared: "Portugal!" Then, I jumped ahead of Serge who always hesitated: "Republica Portugesa, 34,216 square miles, along with the Azores and Madeira, 9,900,000 inhabitants, a corporate republic with its president since 1958, Amerigo Deus Rodriguez Tomas, its capital, Lisbon, its currency, the escudo, and its overseas territories, Cape Verde, Guinea, Sao Tomé, Angola, Mozambique... "

"Well done! Serge, it's your turn: Tanzania!"

"Uhf... Named Tanzania in April, 1966. . . Republic and a member of the Commonwealth, capital, Dar es-Salaam, currency, the African shilling... uhf..."

"Your turn, Aline: Guatemala!"

"Oh, that's easy!"

Aline dropped her book and stretched out on the sand. It was as though she could read them in the clouds, all these striking, odoriferous words swarming with images:

"Republic of Guatemala, 42, 042 square miles, coffee the principal export product, cotton fiber, cocoa, bananas and fruit cultivated by the United Fruit Company, chicle for chewing gum, hard wood, lead, zinc and antinomy. . ."

The atlas was our catechism! We even came to the point where we almost forgot them, where we could no longer imagine them, somewhere, on some out-of-the-way peninsula or in one of the innumerable cities of the world. It had become entrancing, necessary, a kind of feast of memories, an olympiad of words and numbers, a relentless struggle against the nothingness, against fear and loneliness. From time to time, in an effort at cooling this geographic zeal, one or the other of us would bound into the water. This small piece of beach was our section of the Caribbean, our tiny end of the Sahara.

Suddenly, above us on the hill, Julien's silhouette would appear against the pale sky. He'd wave his two arms about, then disappear into the pines. Aline would sigh, then Serge would pick up the net and I'd go along with him to do some fishing, while Aline went to sleep, her head lying beneath the wide open atlas.

No doubt, we were happy that summer, but none of us would have dared to say why or, in our strange innocence, have been able to set a name to that happiness as it flitted by, that summer in the woods, on that silly picnic. "What if they didn't leave on account of us?" we seemed to be thinking. "What if, by abandoning us, they had wanted to free us?"

The old dilapidated *cabane à sucre*. Julien is standing in the doorway. He's talking but I've cut the sound. This cabin was his domain, his refuge, the place where his anger and his nervous attacks died. In the springtime, we used to go up there to collect maple sap and boil up the syrup we'd sell by the roadside under a roof made of planks. We'd have enough to live on then until summer. Julien chopped and carted wood. He was getting strong and we were beginning to be afraid we wouldn't be able to hold him at the height of one of his crises. He had built a still at the back of his cabin. He didn't drink to start with. He made his whisky with uncle Louis-Paul's recipe found in the attic; it was only with the intention of selling it. But he began sampling it, then, to get a bit gay, and then, things progressed very quickly and we would find him dead drunk, in the evening, at the foot of a tree or on his cabin's hard earthen floor. Serge used to say that alcohol did him good. His crises grew farther and farther apart and we shouldn't be alarmed to see him tipsy from time to time. According to Serge, Julien was arriving at some sort of balance. His inner emptiness and the void produced by drunkenness often met head on and this was a good thing. It would pass; Julien was fifteen, he would come to realize. We were letting ourselves be bothered over nothing, Aline and I, mere teenage pranks... Serge used to say:

"Julien is probably more normal than we are. He does his suffering openly!"

That would shut us up, but not for long. Often, in the middle of the night, Aline and I would grab a flashlight and trudge up to his cabin. We were afraid and couldn't get to sleep. What if Julien had put an end to his days with drink, or by shooting himself? The branches crackling under our feet, the cold night air and dark sky, the hooting of owls and the heavy silence of the woods got us all jittery. We would hold hands, like Hansel and Gretel, and that made us laugh and shake all the more. Aline whistled and I would think out loud so as to conjure away our fears:

"Got to do something. We can't keep him here for very long. He needs some sort of care, I don't know, perhaps he's dangerous. . "

"Shut up, Charlie! Shut up!"

34

My words had a worse effect than the darkness, the owls or the silence. Aline would stand stock-still and stare at me then with frightful eyes to get me to keep quiet. Our fear made us see faces in the beams of our flashlights which each of us found quite terrifying. Petrified, we watched the mist formed from our breaths, then, without exchanging another word, we would begin to climb the hill again.

He would be there, stretched out on the moss as though dead. Aline would take him by the legs and I by the shoulders, and we laid him on his bed of spruce boughs at the back of the cabin.

As we were coming back down, dawn was beginning to show through the pinewood. We were pale and tired, with lumps in our throats from all the crazy giggling we had been doing, a common reaction for overwrought young people. Serge was waiting for us in the kitchen.

"Leave him alone! You like to dramatize things, just like all the gossips in town!"

We resented his indifference, in which we could see papa's false serenity, his ability to reason so as not to become emotional. It was then that Aline and I discovered we had a similarly shallow sensibility as well as common obsessions and imaginings which, along with our fears, made for quite a peculiar household. Serge kept saying that we were trying to invent a heroic or baneful destiny for our poor little brother who was merely having an adolescent crisis. He became furious and got very excited when I spoke about mental illness or when, in order to explain Julien's attacks, Aline called to mind Carmen, our mother's "gentle schizophrenia," Serge having made her into a goddess, a martyr and an untouchable. Cool-headed while inwardly seething, we would bicker like specialists, like enraged partisans, with vitriolic harangues followed by sulking sessions that would last the whole afternoon, then we would forget the whole thing by evening, but held fast to our positions until the next time Julien got three sheets to the wind.

My little brother, you were a case, a problem well beyond our years, and especially, well beyond your own.

I press the button and watch you waving your arms and hear you speak of "the smell of maple sap that brought our childhood its fragrance..."

Why has your face taken on that half smile, Charlie, that twisted grimace like a hunter who had gotten lost? Why are your hands continually groping at your neck and through your hair, like nervous little creatures that may have lost their way and can't stay still? Don't answer me, Charlie. I'm delirious. From the top of the apple tree near the shed, I peer at the dark horizon streaked with silver along the hilltops. The wind has fallen and the only thing you can hear is the quiet chirping of the last crickets dazed with fatigue and the summer sun. I'm reading your books, Charlie. Above all, the poems—feverishly. You didn't suspect that, eh, the three of you? That I open your books and read them and perhaps am even drugged by them? Here's another secret, Charlie. (You see, whatever you do, there are always more secrets!) It's your fault all the way! You'll see! It's you and your books that have done it. And those doctors too bared my arm and mixed their chemicals with my blood. Still today, I'm that adolescent filled with anguish and dry as an old tree, being eaten away by some sort of lichen that burns like salt. I know you don't understand, Charlie, and what's more, neither do I.

I've lit a fire with dead branches from our apple trees. I remove my clothes. She's already standing there naked in the fire light. On the dark skin of her belly the flames are tracing out snakes and comets. A great river of stars swims above us. She walks around the fire and it's as though she were dancing. The barn roof glistens with dampness. We are drugged with smoke from the leaves. Do I frighten you, Charlie? Not really, you're acquainted with my fierce energy. For months now, desire has been seeking me out, in the waters, on the sand, in the woods. Her odour mingled with that of the milkweed and coniferous pines ...The world is brutal and so is my madness for her! My desire! My revenge! The jays screech, the whippoorwills send forth their primeval moans as I give myself to her and to the night. I am still a jungle boy. That's what you call me: "the jungle boy." Raised by the animals, having knowledge of their language and knowing nothing of the language of men. But, Charlie, I too am afraid, afraid that little by little you may learn everything ...

Among your books, the only ones that appeal to me are those in which specks of light shine through the debris, books that are unconcerned with conflicts between desire and the mind, those that give as much space to the body's persistence as they do to the head's despair. And

36

I read them outside, sitting at the top of the apple tree or on the little bridge over the creek, or even lying in the field. Words have to flow through my veins to take on meaning. I've dropped several of your books the moment they've asked me to understand things before I could feel them. I've burned a few to start my fires. It's a pleasure to watch their black pages writhing in the flames. I've a feeling I'm watching a bit of your nasty obstinacy and a good deal of my own anger against you disappear in the smoke. In the past, there were no books. Or rather, there was one book, a single one: The Tales. But, as yet, I cannot speak to you of that, my brothers.

Charlie, the doctors were unable to take anything away from me. Whatever they may think, I'm still intact and still "bewitched." They could have driven me insane once and for all, but instead, they only managed to make the voices that I could scarcely hear any more before going to the clinic, clearer, more beautiful and more violent. Yes, I'm talking about that damned inner balance I'll never be able to arrive at, that I never wished for; it has cut all three of you off from joy and terror; it has drawn blue rings around your eyes and impoverished your vision. Nobody knows anything, that's a law we must learn to live with! Some days the great meadow is burning. One morning, the deer come to eat from my hand and, the next, they can no longer be found in the woods...

Charlie, she and I have done what we had to do. My gentle revenge has begun here on this beach. For now, Beauty has gone back to sleep in her cabin.

One December morning, Julien blew into the kitchen dressed in rabbit skins like a *coureur de bois*. There, it's done, he informed us, the *cabane à sucre* was ready, its walls and windows caulked tight for the winter. He came to bid farewell until Christmas. Aline broke out in her barn-owl laugh and Serge smiled shaking his head. I merely said, myself:

"Don't forget, we're counting on you for the wild fowl on Christmas Eve."

Practical and pragmatic as he was, big brother adopted the tone and manner a good father should, not allowing himself to be particularly put out by some further trifle. But our Radisson was smelling fiercely of gin from his still and was cavorting about the kitchen looking for supplies so as to be able to hold out until that holy night. I was wild with rage though I let nothing show. Oh! how I resented them then, for having left us Julien to bring up and to watch over! For forcing us to cope with his madness as well as our own powerlessness! The festivities of Christmas were taking on all the hues of Lent, Christ's Passion, the crown of thorns, the gall, with Aline and Serge, my two Pontius Pilates washing their hands of it all. For me, "the elder Christ," these images from the Gospel were quite devastating. Given the frequent visits to church papa had forced upon his three older children, this is practically all that they had left me with: scenes of horror, the Way of the Cross, my first film, in its bronze and gilded frame, with, thrown in, the recurring feeling that life might be nothing but a long Easter vigil with resurrection being in no way assured. (Indeed, the more I think about it, the more I realize that I wanted to make films so as to blot out this first masterpiece that had been molded and made mine, in spite of myself: that haunting, cruel and unrivaled Way of the Cross!).

We were about to live three long weeks without seeing Julien. First of all, everything was frozen solid, then it snowed so heavily that the road leading up to the *cabane à sucre* became impassable, even on snowshoes. We would get buried up to our thighs for the clearing and fields had turned into a sea of powdery snow. Serge and I chopped wood until our arms were ready to fall off to keep the fire going while Aline kept knitting away endlessly, making scarves and tuques. She succeeded in putting together, with bits of carpet and table cloth, a large quilt which kept all three of us warm in the evenings on the living room couch, reading books and beginning all over again the trips and distances covered on their "flight into Egypt," as Aline called it. Pale and shivering under the patchwork quilt that smelled like a wet dog, like innocent saints, we tried to follow the shepherd's star that was tracing its way across the sky without ever stopping above the manger where father and mother were no doubt shivering away much as we were. In the glimmer of Christmas candles found in the attic, (the electricity was often off for entire days, that winter), with crowns woven in vine stems and sparkling wreathes, we lived this Advent period, feebly maintaining our hopes for a miracle, their return coinciding with the mystery of the birth of a tiny God in the straw. We used to pray, rediscovering the frantic fervour of feverish nights years before when, along with mama's, we would make our voices rise towards an abstract and benevolent heaven, begging Jesus, Mary and Joseph to transform this world into a paradise. We promised that we would be more generous than Melchior, Gaspard and Balthazar at the feet of the Infant-King, offering Him our hearts forever, that we would be wiser than the angels throughout our lands and warmer than the ox and the donkey in the stable, if the miracle were actually to happen:——if they, our parents, were to appear in the doorway on Christmas eve, ragged and repentant. Aline read aloud *The Little Match Girl* and we wept, all three of us huddling close together under the quilt.

Without Julien, we became sentimental and fidgety. But what was he doing up there in his cabin while we were preparing to spend our Christmas as poor little orphans shivering from cold and grief? According to Serge: "He goes trapping, he eats and he sleeps." For Aline: "He's meditating, he's in communion with the spirit of the frozen earth." For me: "He gets drunk and can't forget how monstrous he is. "Decidedly, only Julien can rouse us up and plunge us into quite as convincing a state of anguish. It was we who were the parents and our little one had run away. He wasn't far away; yet, for us, he was lost——" the Julien mystery, "as Serge called it. It's only today, before these scenes from my aborted film (I wanted to call it *Julien the Magnificent*), that I'm beginning to understand, or maybe, at least to surmise. What if he's been "putting on an act" all those years? What if he became entangled in his own game, in his own fairy tale, until it drove him mad? Having recognized the despair in all our fiddling with maps, our books and our scientific talk, what if he had decided to make a sacrifice of himself? In the tragedy of Grand Remous, it was he who was the shadowy figure, the maniac, the one whose behaviour was questionable and quite extraordinary! Was it just to prevent the four of us from dying from those destitute conditions we were living in? His cabin, his solitary retreat, his "*coureur des bois*" game, it was all probably a diversion, a myth, a metaphor, a dangerous sublimation, but one inspired by a definite affection. There were those many times when he would say, for example, opening his eyes wide and with a comical shrug of the shoulders:

"Guys like me are necessary, maybe the world need fireflies in the depths of winter. . ."

The world, that meant us! A sinking world. Julien cast his glimmerings, radiant and demented as they were, upon a reality which would most assuredly have crumbled without them. We didn't understand, we weren't able. Our furious search for the reasons, motives and explanations for everything—their departure, our state of abandonment, and above all, my dear little brother, your misdemeanours—prevented us from really knowing you, made us believe you were crazy, Julien, a lunatic awed by grandeur and sorcery. With you, my brother, how were we to know? But perhaps all these thoughts that have come to me more recently are, themselves, nothing but faint glimmerings—a need for some tale which would be somewhat different from the one I have clung to so vigorously and that I most feared to be true, for in this one, I "knew" you were mad, that is to say, chosen by madness and not choosing this madness yourself because of... yes, because of love!

Faithful to his promise, Julien came home with gifts at Christmas time: three statuettes he had carved from cedar wood. Two Adams and an Eve, naked and with open arms, their three tinseled heads closely resembling our own. If the three statuettes were set together, we held in our hands a small chubby tree with drooping limbs. We fingered it in turn, giggling with fascination, speculating on its possible meanings, since we were convinced Julien wanted to "send us a message." This effort was futile: the tree remained a small smooth and gracious mystery lying there in the palms of our hands.

Ten years later, while traveling towards the South still on their traces, I saw this tree on the outskirts of the town of Savannah, an immense one with all its leaves blowing in the wind. It was a tulip tree from Virginia.

In the village, they call him the ogre of Grand Remous. I watch him scaling the long ladder that leans against the barn's sky light. When lightning flashes across the dark sky, he catches it in his hand and laughs like a mad horse as he looks at me.

"Did you see me, eh, did you see me, Tom Thumb?"

He wavers at the top of the ladder, he's going to fall!——and he laughs, he roars with laughter! I leave my hiding place under the porch... It's not raining, the water's coming in sheets, just like under a waterfall. I approach the ladder. I want to help him, I want to kill him, I don't know what I want! The ladder sways and Trinité bellows with laughter!

"You're afraid, eh, you're afraid, Tom Thumb!"

A ball of fire streaks from the sky. I'm holding the ladder. I want to help! Trinité shouts:

"Get away, you're going to make me fall, Tom Thumb, you scamp!"

I saw him, I saw him vanish with the fire in the sky! I was still holding the ladder, I was gripping the ladder and now, up above, there was a reddish flame lighting up the sky light, but no Trinité! I swear, my brothers, I saw him flying off with that fire across the sky! I didn't do anything, I was holding the ladder, I wanted to help him!

Oh, of course, the ogre had his revenge, he came back. After that night at the dam, he came back to life. He wanted to devour me, and you as well. He wanted to get Grand Remous away from us! I had to kill him a second time. Trinité had to die again, he had to! Oh, my brothers, I still can't talk to you about all that ...

She told me: "You're not crazy!" She didn't tell me, like the doctors: "But ogres don't exist!"

I walk through the pinewood with the large story book under my arm. This evening, I'm going to answer Irene's questions, read her stories and talk about Trinité. Maybe I'll sleep in her cabin, that small cottage, the ogre's former hideaway. Now everything's behind me: my life as a persecuted little Tom Thumb, my wait, my error, the clinic, the doctors, that terrible hundred years of sleep! She will understand that the ogre existed and that I already paid for that night and for the other one, the one by the dam! She too has had her ogre, so she'll understand. And so will you, my brothers, you'll come to understand as well!

I walk out among the birches, at the top of the rock. The moon shines on the water in the dam ...

This morning in my mail there's a light blue envelop bearing two immense stamps representing the sand dunes on Cape Cod. I tear it open and a scribbler whose cover I recognize——a little boy fishing off the end of a wooden dock with water of an unreal blue falls onto my knees. The loose page of a note pad is stapled to it. I recognize, of course, Serge's handwriting.

Hello, Charlie!

Found this scribbler while tidying up old affairs. *Old secrets, ancient horrors!* You who want to understand and to know so much, look all this over, *lonesome worrier.*

I'm staying here for the winter. My friend——the same one for eight months, *would you believe it?*——is an artist, a painter. This terrible illness constrains your brother to be faithful and, gosh, he's getting used to it, the poor fellow! He recreates things in his own way, high in colour, decadence and radiant beaches and, as everyone here showers him with: "*I love your work!*", we're digging in here and everything's going for the best, or just about. Oh yes! the proof is now made of what you always prophesied, dear Elder, by this I mean that I'm becoming the biggest gigolo in all America, and *I don't care anymore about it!*

No trace of the folks, if you want to know. Neither on the sands of the vast beaches, nor in the waves, nor on the hotel terraces, nor in tourist rooms, nor on the bridges of the yachts where the *beautiful people* on the coast lounge about. Forget about it, Charlie! That's what I always preached, didn't I? Pure and simple forgetting. I don't always manage every day myself, but *so what?*

Good luck with the next movie and don't go crazy, yourself, with... all that! How did they say it, in bygone days? "Glide, glide and don't lean too hard!", or something like that?

> *Farewell and love*
> *my deep and profound brother,*
> Serge

My young brother, *as usual*, terrified but light-hearted. I open the scribbler. On the first page, there's Aline's writing: "Serge's dreams, spring and winter, 1965." I feel suddenly very warm; heavy trembles make the hairs bristle all over me. Serge's dreams: Aline had him relate them and she noted them down scrupulously in this scribbler with the little fisherman on the cover. We used to claim, Aline and I, that Serge's unconscious spoke like an omen. He, the *cool*, nonchalant, "sidetracked" adolescent, that tender madman, incurably in love with mama, had dreams in which would appear "the prisoner who turned away from escaping." His fantasies, noted down by Aline and then, attentively studied, seemed to us to be triggering a "recovery process leading to a cure," or so we read in one of papa's books.

Aline's Notebook

Serge's first dream: "Mama's bones."

All three of us are sitting (Julicn isn't with us) on a moss-covered rock overlooking the dam. Aline's crying Charles plunges his arm into the water and, one by one, pulls up mama's bones, all gray, dull and lying there loose. He fishes them out, one by one, unhurriedly. He murmurs: "I knew it! I knew it!", and he seems very calm. Suddenly, I find myself back in our bedroom. Julien's there, sitting on my bed, smiling as he spins our globe of the world. I look for my shoes so I can leave but I can't find them. Aline says: "You can't walk, why shoes?" And all three of you laugh, and myself, I fall, I fall into a void...

Aline and I would rack our brains and page through papa's books trying to explain these dreams that troubled us much more than they did the dreamer, himself. Serge, slumped down on the couch, used to recite them like a medium in a trance. Once the dream had been revived, he would shrug his shoulders, as though suddenly awake again, and run off to play outside leaving us to our frenzied conjecture. Of course, we would never be able to figure out these dreams completely. We could get no further than irrelevant, anecdotal and outlandish interpretations and ended up going along with Serge's ravings with all their violent twists and turns. A sacred fear prevented us from dealing with that horrid event, the original catastrophe, their departure. Our inquiries should have been made with shrewdness and insight which, of course, were things we didn't have. Nevertheless, we wanted to understand, to be aware of what had occurred. We wanted to know the real causes of what we called our "fourfold ailment." But we lacked the love, cut off from us like an electric current, that would have helped us to immerse ourselves in our various dreads with greater trust. However, once we had begun, we couldn't turn back, and much less so when we thought of giving up our analyzing sessions which, through a lack of clearheadedness, brought us to discover a startling complicity that helped pass the time. And then, we were probably slowly coming to understand something we would never be able to put into words, that is to say, that we were perhaps not only the victims but also, to a certain extent, the authors of our own miseries and that often we do not suffer certain pangs without unconsciously having provoked them in the first place.

The cold made Aline and I huddle deeper under the covers, sometimes until late into the night. Daily life became an abstraction. Serge slogged away all alone at the wood pile and cooked suppers that neither of us were able to digest. When we probed deeply, memories of our parents were the only things that came back to us (Aline in particular could ramble on about them forever); they were things we wanted to forget. A sort of diffuse all-embracing sorrow prevented us from sleeping or from stirring about in that big bed. Once again, we were abandoned, lost and given over, unable to resist, to a kind of dizzy whirl our brother's dreams swept us into. He was, in spite of himself, a psychic medium who refused suffering, who found relief from his demons each morning by telling us about them and who cut wood behind the house or brewed up pots of grub in the kitchen, just to draw us away from our empty dreaming.

Why has this scribbler come back to me? What are Serge's dreams, those old ramblings from a earlier world, doing back in my life today? What can I still search for or hope to find? A film that misfired, scraps of memory, faint clues, jumbled bits of dreams and an affection that came rather late: these are the only paths that might lead me back to Grand Remous.

I stop, as though short of breath. And, just as I thought, it's Serge's voice I hear mumbling somewhere away off.

"Get outside! Go for a walk and stop thinking about ... all those things!"

He would say "All those things!" with an immense swing of his arms, meaning: make a clean sweep of it all, that pile of rot, that inextricable muddle, that dog's dinner!

One evening, coming out of the book room after another one of our sessions at interpreting Serge's dreams, we opened the door on Julien who had quite visibly been spying on Aline and me. He blushed, then smiled before bellowing my way :

"A young prince in love is always valiant!"

Then, lowering his voice and this time towards Aline:

"But little Tom Thumb didn't reveal anything of what he knew to his brothers!"

With these sibylline words, he turned his back and strode off towards his bedroom, whistling. Aline, without looking at me—but I could feel she was trembling and uneasy—murmured:

"What did he mean?"

Obviously, I didn't know what he meant. I still don't know. Whether all or any of it. What had he heard behind that door? What did he know? What part was pure comedy in the role he played as a clear-sighted savage? What did he expect us to understand, then, with his occasional stunning replies and everlasting monk-like silences? Were the poisons of madness slowly coursing their way through him? And even today, what's he trying to make us understand?

It was that evening that Aline pronounced that very adult and bitter phrase that, afterwards, I would always find unsettling:

"All the four of us are inseparable, yet opposed!"

I did know what that meant! We all had a single destiny, a single life to share, a single soul dwelling in four bodies, four beings possessing the same body, etc., and all that *mumbo-jumbo*, as Serge would say, our American friend, our false exile.

47

No one comes to our aid, Charlie. I'm ten years old and for the first time I see the ogre Trinité again. He steps across hills with a single stride, his footprints cover an entire clearing. I'm quite a little fellow, my legs are numb from having sat too long on that mossy rock behind the barn. I first notice his shadow in the waters of the creek, then his foot leaping over the stream like lightning. I can hear his breath that's like a hurricane in my ears, and his grumbling voice that rumbles like thunder to the very depths of the pinewood: "Get away from here, so I don't tread on you...!"

I never talk to you about the ogre, Charlie. I question the bushes and trees. I feel the wild flowers staring at me, frightened for me. I lie down in the green hay, close my eyes, then a butterfly comes and brushes against my ear to remind me that it's all my fault, that the ogre Trinité is after me, that one day he'll find me and it will be your turn next!

I remain faithful to the plants and animals that protect me from him. I live according to their council and they help me in moments of trouble. It's never a person who intercedes on my behalf with the ogre. No one comes to help us!

Through the underbrush in the maple tree grove, I follow a deer that has been wounded by one of my 30/30 bullets. For three long days, I glue my ear to the elms and birches and pick up each of his wild efforts to dash away. Then, I see him standing there frozen with pain, rubbing his flank gently against the soft face of a rock, then bounding off this way and that. I keep following his tracks. Every time he stops to rub himself again, I see the spot where his wound has bled upon the bark or stone. When I finally manage to get close, he's exhausted. It's because he is about to die that he lets me stroke him. It's then I know that I am like him and I weep as I slide my hand over his hide soaked with blood.

No, I'm not mad! One day, maybe, you will understand, all by yourselves.

If I've accepted the doctors' treatments, it's because I knew I was going to die. The ogre has caught up with me again. No one comes to help us!

I can't sleep. The window's open, a light snow is whipping about and there's a smell of damp earth and withered plants, the very odours of autumn at Grand Remous. I turn the pages of Aline's scribbler, unable to decide whether or not to go on reading Serge's nightmares (there are more than fifty pages, all in Aline's compact handwriting!). I'm not able to watch the film either. I feel I'm somehow stopped, that I'm trembling on the edge of something ... Suddenly, I know why, I remember Alexis Korba and a feverish telephone call, right here in this apartment where I took refuge ten years ago:

"Hello!"

There was crackling on the line; it was like a cloud of frenzied cicadas trying to let me in on a precious secret. And then, a tiny voice that I recognized right away:

"Hello, there!"

"Aline?"

"It's me!"

"My young sister! Where are you?"

"Still on the island of Crete. Zorba hasn't come back, so I'm waiting for him!"

Aline was laughing behind the crackling. Zorba! Our master, our real father!" Aline's bedside book and to me, a major film."Woe to him who has not within himself the source of happiness! Woe to him who wants to please others! Woe to him who does not feel that this life and the next one are but one!" We used to repeat, after Zorba, running through the streets in the town: "I'm covered with wounds that have healed, that's why I'm able to go on!" Zorba, the splendid orphan, the free being par excellence, he who, each day, saw everything as though for the first time. It's he who urged us to leave, who chased us away, so to speak, from Grand Remous. We had bought the records of the music from the film and used to dance entire evenings to the sounds of a santuri, our heads on fire, forgetting their travels and thinking of our own. Sating "our soul that is body, our body that is soul," we used get drunk on Zorba, talk about that Great Folly, our new name for their departure, their desertion, and dance on and on to mournful melodies: yes, life

49

flowed between our fingers and neither heaven nor hell existed. We would dance until our backs ached. Serge banged on the floor in his bedroom, shouting: "Stop it! Stop it!" But we kept dancing until, just like Zorba on the sands of his beach in Crete, our bodies would collapse onto the living room couch. And I would shout:

"Play on, Zorba, play on!"

Aline would weep and dance all by herself when I fell asleep on the couch: the wild beast had given up. The next day, I would awaken, still excited, with Aline huddled against me. Then, we would start over; I put the record back on and once again we would see the beaches of Crete, the great Anthony Quinn waving his arms about the Greek sky, and Aline would pick up her book again and read:

"Life is like that, checkered, incoherent, indifferent, perverse and pitiless!"

Rushing down stairs, Serge would stop the music and stare at us like some aghast dispenser of justice.

"Your Zorba talks just like our brother whom you call crazy! Come now, let's be a bit rational! You make a god out of one of them and you want to lock the other one up!"

Completely winded from our dancing, we would look at him as though he was someone from another planet. Then, we'd go off into mad laughter, put the record back on and begin dancing again. We were a bit ashamed, of course. (Serge certainly had reason on his side, but what was reason?) We didn't feel like losing our passion for Zorba and returning to terror and despair. We kept on dancing and time passed harmlessly by, as had the months and years for *Zorba the Greek* in his Cretan palace. It was in December, 1968 (here comes the sun, the dawn of the age of Aquarius was rising, far off over there), we had just left Grand Remous, leaving the land to Julien, the savage, we were going out into the world: we were about to do what they had done!

"You didn't meet them somewhere up on the Acropolis or at the ruins of Cnossus?"

"No more traces of them, Charlie, than of Dionysos or of Bouboulina!"

Aline still had her owlish laugh, a bit subdued though, now. In three phrases, probably rehearsed out loud before the telephone call, she described the beaches of Crete invaded by hippies searching for some absurd and unjustifiable exhilaration "and spoke of having eaten a peach as large as a melon that very afternoon, and this had given her a desire, an intense desire to talk about her poor nostalgic older brother, closed away in some shabby studio endeavoring to master those machines that were some day destined to obey him and to produce a masterpiece which would reduce *Zorba the Greek* to the level of a third rate film in black and white. No more suffering in her voice, merely a calm and composed irony, the quiet bitterness of an adult girl, alone and wandering about the world. And then, quite abruptly, came the terrible question:

"Any news of Julien? Did you go and see him at the clinic?"

Suddenly, I was overcome with panic again, a sort of rapid violent choking that left me quite powerless as soon as I was reminded of that clinic. Aline was waiting at the other end of the line, she too stifling her breathing. Probably, she had guessed I was having a "stroke" as we used to say in the past when giving burlesque treatment to papa's dramatic phrases. I hadn't gone to see him for some time, but the doctor had phoned:

"What did he say?"

"Oh, nothing. Evidently Julien has been talking about Trinité Lauzon again, of the road to the mansion and the guards asleep for a hundred years."

"What are you talking about?"

I explained to Aline that the doctor was worried and phoned me from time to time to ask: "the giant Trinité," does that mean anything to you?" I spoke to him about big Trinité Lauzon's accident that had impressed Julien so much when he was little. The doctor sighed. I did too. Surely, Julien was trying to tell us something. But what? The doctor sighed again and hung up. Aline gave a frightened little laugh into the phone:

'He's acting again. He's pretending, isn't that it?"

"I don't know, Aline. I'm often quite afraid."

Another great sigh and some more crackling, perhaps it was Cretan insects.

"Me too, Charlie, but what else were we to do?"

"Don't know."

"I mean… Oh, Charlie, I'm guilty, you're guilty, it's all our fault!"

"Don't say that! Eat another melon-peach, go and jump in the waves and don't think about him, nor about us, nor about them, Aline! Do you remember? "The earth's heart split open, the very gentle oriental poison spread. I could feel all the fibers rotting inside me…"

"… that still bound me to virtue and to fear.'Zorba!'"

"Zorba, you're right! Our brother will come out of it, you'll see!"

Our trusting and protective big brother, infatuated with movie making, forever our blameless elder!

I no longer know what Aline's last words were. I can only remember the santuri music. In fact, after my sister's telephone call, I put on that record and danced all by myself, in my room on Gaspé Street, desiring, just like Zorba had done, to plunge my head into the sea ("I'm on fire, I have to put myself out! ").

At that time, I was making my first film, a flimsy haunting story about a case of mistaken identity. I wanted to come out of obscurity at any cost and exorcise my holy fears: I felt I needed everything and yet, I didn't know what to do with it all. Unlike Aline, I hadn't been able to get close to the sun and the sea. I had to work and to redeem myself. In the end, I was the other half of Zorba, his *dark side*: the trapped creator. For her part, Aline continued her geography cure, whether for better or for worse, like some aimless pilgrimage.

Often, I would take the car and drive north. Would I head for Grand Remous or for the clinic? Would I go and see the ruins of our home or our devastated brother? In the end, I made an about-face, returning to the city and my work. It was all quite impossible.

And, whether feeling thoroughly stultified or, quite on the contrary, bursting with hope, I drove, without being too aware either of the road or of my fear, to Maniwaki rather than Julien, it was the doctor who came and meet me on the clinic's huge steps. He shook my hand, smiled and said :

"Your brother refuses to see you... You know, it's probably better that way."

I didn't ask any questions, didn't go any farther; it was as though I were indifferent. I slowly went back down the steps and noticed Julien in the park, his back leaning against the trunk of a tree. After Grand Remous, his attacks, the past, the three of us, his madness—nothing seemed to disturb him any more. I got back in my car and drove back to the city, absolutely lifeless, absolutely beaten.

Only once did he see me, and then, he gave me one of his big waves, the kind he used to make when he would spot us from the top of the hill sitting on the little beach before our books and maps. A great wave to say farewell, a wave that was resigned, solemn and peaceful. Was it the farewell of a man who was drowning or of someone who is watching the other sink?

Are you at the center of everything, then, my anchorite brother?

I'm like a heap of burning embers in a cold and windy night, Charlie. While I can feel the anguish edging threateningly in on me, I remain calm, nonetheless. The fact is I've come a long way and the devil knows which way I'm going. Don't you see, the most important thing is to be alive and to know that you are. People's words are always muddled, and then, we prefer believing our own eyes rather than figuring things out with our minds. I'm not the craziest of the crazies, Charlie. Sometimes it's all quite clear: what the catbird tells me, for example, the one perched on the highest branch of the cedar that looks down on our bedrooms. The scraping of its boughs wakes us up on windy nights and the rest of you begin talking so as not to give way to your fears, while, myself, I listen, follow and am not able to repeat everything the catbird's mewing reveals to me. Charlie, I too receive the impulses controlling the bird's nerves! The bird is saying: "I'm not blessed with a very long life span, I'm created over and over again, day by day, minute by minute, in some miraculous way!" That's what the catbird tells me and, Charlie, I believe it. Because I too am created over and over every second, just like the bird, and I cry out within my own self for the miracle to continue, for heaven to let me live on... How can I explain it? Nothing here, at home, has a talent for words. But the birds are the most talkative, the most inspired and perhaps the most troubled. In spring, it's the bodies of the thrushes and orioles that have the strongest impulses. In winter, it's those of the crows and blue jays which I feed, just to help the miracle along, by sprinkling sunflower seeds out on logs. Charlie, without the slightest hesitation, I can identify the soul that lies within them just by the timbre of their voices, by their phrasing, by the melodies or screeches that escape from their throats. The gray jay, for example, with its whistling wee-wee that carries quite far, speaks continually of exile. It's full of yearning, like Aline, and I often believe I hear our sister's voice, like that of a perched bird, telling me about her wanderings and her endless quest. The wren's tiny explosive chimp-chimp and also the nervous flutterings of its tail held high remind me of Serge and his impatient twitching and, perhaps it's actually Serge himself, Serge's soul! What I mean is, have Serge and the wren possibly the same soul, are they effected by the same tormenting impulses, the same annoying desire? You're the towhee with its rust-colored flanks that constantly digs at the soil with its two feet scratching away simultaneously, and whose song strangely varies from drink-ioor-teewee to to-wee or chewink. It sometimes says yes and no, both at the same time, but it appears to be always happy about it, about its vitality and its perplexed manner, its odd love for riddles, resembles your own—of this, there's no doubt.

It is not always possible to cast off boredom, pain and fatigue or to remain aloof from death. You, Aline and also Serge want to follow closely the cadence of civilization, to go on ceaselessly fighting earth, air, fire and water, for you are heroes: according to you, the world has to have meaning, "everything has to lead somewhere!" You want to be involved, to meddle in everything, in order not to be alone with the world. For me, none of all this counts, since I'm mad, since I've done what I've done! Maybe the three of you don't know how to take in impulses? Oh yes, you do! Serge in the creek, flowing along confidently, fish-like, with the current, having himself become a course in the stream, skimming the reeds and mossy rocks, skillful and sure of himself, fearless and above reproach. Aline, dipping her brushes in the runny saffron yellow, liquefied gold, carrying it over onto the rough clay surface to make her sunflowers, receiving impulses and transmitting them, handing her flesh and her soul over to these impulses and exposing her wounds much as a butterfly shows its markings! And you, Charlie, lying stretched out on your back in the sun on that little beach, your body all brown and your heart melting, suddenly slowed by the patient movement of the galaxies, receiving the reddish light from that morning's brand new world, your tongue rolling in a juicy saliva, already creating poems, as your brain exhales new images! You don't need any rolls of film, nor a screen, nor a projector, Charlie! And if I disturb you,——yes, often I do it on purpose it's to see you suddenly pale, grimacing and sorry-looking, and then, I know: even you, Charlie, a disconnected current, if the impulses don't reach you, again you become lonely, sad and forsaken, rushing headlong towards death with your rather unaware intelligence. However, I know very well, Charlie, that you couldn't care less about winning or losing! I know that you're going to get angry, lie, speak with those old words, and that you never fail to come out with a: "Julien, you're bothering me, stop spying on me!" And then, turning away from me and with your head thrown back: "You, you can't really understand..." But yes, I can! It's fear that has taken hold of you once again! If only you knew how well I understand you!

For the second time, the ogre Trinité is dead, my brother! When I walked back out of the cabin up there where she lives on the first morning, I immediately spotted his large body stretched out on the meadow—a gigantic shadow, a skeleton looking like the trunk of an immense oak tree struck by lightening. Then I understood, Charlie, I understood that it was I who had killed him. But there was no triumph in the ogre's death: it was a murder of which, nonetheless, I wasn't guilty. Simply because he was discouraged with being monstrous for no good reason, the ogre fell, emptied of his powers, like a statue that had split in the freezing cold, just as, in the past, he had vanished in passing storms. That morning, I drew myself up with all my newfound height and then I saw my shadow on the ground, immense and flimsy as it was, wavering in the wind. Now, I'm the ogre, with my head in the clouds and my feet in the dam's flowing waters, breathing in great gasps of air, happy with my newly found power for living without terrifying anyone or anything. Do you understand? I no longer have any reason for drinking, for besotting myself or for striking out in an effort to quiet my fears! If you so wish, no more reason for being crazy! Charlie, the ogre is dead!

Aline's Notebook

Serge's thirty-seventh dream

The three of us, Charlie, Aline and I, are flying above the pinewood, towards the dam. We know our wings are frail and that the rising sun will melt them if we don't hurry. (No doubt, here, a hint of the Icarus legend read by Charles, last night, before nodding off). We fly down, myself in front, to a mossy rock near the falls, where Julien is resting. Aline slowly approaches Julien, his body lying there naked and quite still. Is he dead? Is he asleep? By his side, there's a pile of unraveled strips, like curly lengths of birch bark. (Julien loves to shroud himself in these strips and play dead from time to time, just to frighten us.) Charlie suddenly seizes two of these bark strips and by rubbing them together, he makes a shape appear, first of all, a hazy one in smoke, then, slowly, this turns into mama's face. With a burst of laughter, Julien then leaps forward and, with his fist which has turned solid, (papa's own solid frame being away in the shed) smashes the hardened face which crumbles like dust upon the grass. Then, naked and trembling, Julien stares at all three of us, as radiant as a sun—one of Aline's suns—and spouts:

"I'm the master of this secret! Who wants to follow me without any further ado?"

And it is I who answer all alone and very loud so as to be heard above the uproar from the dam:

"I do."

Their wings having melted, Aline and Charlie, look at me with their pale and grimacing features, as though I was the biggest traitor in the world. Then Aline says in a faint voice:

"We have to return to the earth for all the visitors are leaving!"

How is it then we didn't understand this transparent, prophetic dream? Julien would go crazy and you, Serge, since your fear was so great, you would choose to forget. As for Aline and myself, we would come back to earth, "for all the visitors were leaving!"

Memory's Old Couch
(Aline)

Everything began the morning I came back down from the hill. Whether it be the beaches of Crete, the banks of Guatemalan rios, the pearl dust of the Caribbean or the reddish sands of the Sierra. San Pedro where I am today, no place in the world has ever made me forget that golden stretch of cove at Grand Remous, our little beach where I walked upon the sand, that morning, as nimbly as a ghost returning from the dead.

I had just passed two days and a night up on the hill, sleeping in the sun or under the stars on a moss-covered rock, sometimes dozing and at other times awake, but forever traveling in memories that I took for dreams. My arms and legs were trembling but the cold had nothing to do with it. A violent current was passing through me and I was tormented with shocks in no way related to the soil below me, although, several years later, in Guatemala, I was to sense once again the very same horrible trembling when, one night, the earth opened up beneath an encampment where I was sleeping with some gringos, more surprised than I by this "previously experienced" cataclysm. In all the heavy shaking, my store of memories had come tumbling out.

I remembered every life, first of all our own, then those of Georges and Carmen, and finally, all those who had lived before us in this heavenly and hellish spot. No matter how often I told myself (while my body was shivering at some far removed point in time) that I was inventing it all, that Julien's madness had caught up with me, that it was my state of excitement and helplessness that was giving me this witch's sense of enchantment, I knew that I remembered, that I had become, though unconsciously and without wanting to, someone who honoured memories and was obsessed by them, someone aware of all the adventures, dramas and accidents that had taken place at Grand Remous.

It's because I had become too good a listener. I had developed an uncommon ear or as Serge would say, I was "a remarkable memorizer, a divine soothsayer." Tell me an inch and I'd discover a mile all by myself. And of course, I wasn't too often wrong, jumping ahead of the story teller and, with my glib tongue, pouring out the rest of his story in a torrent of words. How was it possible? Had I already seen and heard everything? Had I always been there with my eyes open wide and clear hearing; wasn't this even before having existed in the world, listening while still obscurely ensconced inside Carmen, our mother, and even before this, in that original nothingness? A memory that's not only historic, but pre-historic! A phenomenal marvel!

Everything came to me, or should I say came back to me, as easily as the stream of water—cold, impetuous and unconscious that was coursing its way down the hill between the flat smooth boulders. Lying on my rock shaken with spasms, distrustful, yet sure of the flow of my memories, some of which were recent, while others were antediluvian, drugged with the aroma of the pines and the song of the wind in their branches, I rushed across time, across the seasons, catching upon people and scenes as I went, just as long ago, when very little, I would run into onlookers bunched together at the village fair behind the church. It was too much, yet it wasn't enough! When it came down to it, I wanted to do everything, see everything and not miss a trick! Nevertheless, I could feel that something essential was getting away from me, even though my memory was working away unerringly, fiercely, relentlessly, retracing its steps, beginning this or that episode over again, re-imagining some rain storm or other, or mama's anger, or the shadow of that stray dog, the one who bit Serge—did he have rabies?—against the wall of the shed, that ghostly shadow that used to keep mama awake all night in the grips of an apocalyptic and quite romantic terror, as were all the emotions of this lady who liked to devour eccentric tales. This ghostly figure would even make me get up myself, put on my rubber boots and go down and trudge about our vegetable garden. I had to know, had to be sure: was it really that wild dog, the last off-spring of that last generation of German shepherds once raised by our uncle Louis-Paul who, that very year, had been living in exile with his wife for seventeen years in Albany, New York, where he, the best dog trainer in all America, was now putting white wolves through their paces for the Vargas circus. The fear of this dog, a savage beast that had become more dangerous than a wolf banished from its clan, the night's heavy cold, the absurdity of my lonely jaunt into the middle of a garden teaming with groundhogs and snakes, the memory or the imagining of horrible scenes——those battles with monsters found in the novels Charles was so fond of, and that he would force me to read in order to "tame my terrors"—nothing of all this would prevent me from wading about in the muddy swamp behind our shed until finally the beam of my flashlight would capture that fixed stare, those two menacing fiery eyes, those fangs glistening in the quivering light beam that I held upon that oblong terrifying head, a face which I found, suddenly, no longer frightening. Yes, it was he. The animal had indeed this beige mark on its chest and paws with six nails that uncle Louis called "lynx paws." And I would walk back to the house, relieved, shivering, soaked with dew up to my waist and not at all troubled by that fierce dog who had run off into the swamp after having stared unflinchingly upon the innocent apparition that I was, as though it were something quite normal, even predictable, the booted girl with the long memory who came to see him just to know he was there and who, now, could return home soothed and untroubled. At breakfast the next morning, she would tell her next of kin, sitting quietly eating their porridge and maple syrup, the story of uncle Louis-Paul's last dog, making them laugh and watch and listen attentively, going even so far as to describe the German shepherds' kennel of some fifteen years before on the riverside, the growling and wild smell of the animals frightened by the night, papa's moments of despondency and mama's "German shepherd" neurosis, never running short of details which, in reality, I couldn't remember!

"But this child's a marvel!"

It was papa, especially, who couldn't get over it: uncle Louis-Paul had gone away from Grand Remous eighteen months after my birth!

That morning, I got up from my "philosopher's stone" as Charlie was to name it later, with my bones aching and my muscles all stiff, famished and my mind a total blank. The weather was mild, the sun's rays came piercing through the pines. We were finally at the height of summer and for the time being I was given my freedom. I walked towards the river, winding my way between two rows of apple trees which had returned to their original wild state; some small apples were already dangling from them like tiny silent bells. I plucked one down and bit into it, sitting in the wind on our sandy beach. The little apple's acidity reminded me that I was still alive and still at Grand Remous. I recognized Charlie and Serge's light footprints still fresh on the glistening shore. They had been looking for me and here I was, coming back towards them, little Aline, emaciated, fragile and dazed with the sharpness of her memories, her nerves drained and, what was most disturbing, thoroughly mute. This was quite so, I wouldn't say a thing. Slumping down in silence on that old broken-down couch on the porch, I only had enough strength to smear antiseptic cream on my insect bites and to stroke the cat, who didn't recognize me either. How could I explain this? You're jinxed, a nasty miracle changes you and makes you take a path you believe reserved for someone who's either mad or wise, for either Julien or for Charlie but not for you! And here you are, meek, exhausted and no longer having anything to go on but your inspiration and an absurd confidence: since you didn't say no, since you didn't back away, since your body had begun to obey, everything will be fine now! But where should I start? How must I arrange these phantoms and describe their adventures, how should I set my weird store of memories in motion once again without having this raging swirl drive me out of my mind. Both inside me and around me, the silence was buzzing with life like a swarm of wasps. There was silence... then, suddenly, I thought: "There, that's both the way it is and the way it always will be! On certain days, I won't speak: I'll just remember! To my brothers, I'll be thinking things over, as stubbornly

64

as a mule, I'll even pout!" There was no need to inform them about my having to remember and that I was now a great chronicler, a "memory gatherer" who wasn't to be intruded upon. *"Do not disturb,"* Serge would say, "Miss Aline's feeling low!" All right then, I'd get feeling low, I'd sulk if need be! Later, I'd travel and pretend to forget, to find enjoyment and to make my life. I would find peace. That is to say that, my memories would be at rest. This stubborn silence was the price to be paid if I wanted to stop the capricious goddess of vague recollections from driving me insane as well!

Oh, I'll let them in a bit on what's going on from time to time! I'll tell them, in a voice made hoarse from long periods of silence, the story of the village fire or, pressed by their numerous questions, about Trinité Lauzon going all numb up there in his "grotto" on top of our barn, a story that Julien knows better than I, however, because he saw the giant Trinité "leaping into the sky!" But I'll keep the more magical accounts to myself, those that would resist time and still have their horrifying effect: most particularly those episodes about our parents' past, the probable reasons, motives, or at least, certain hints leading to their departure, which remained the keystone, the heart, the driving force behind that typhoon-like wave of memories that engulfed me without warning whenever and wherever it wished. Just as, later, the scrupulous transcription of Serge's dreams, that disquieting undercurrent with its abrasive effects, even though it might not lead to a cure, it might perhaps serve to explain at least the sickness brought on by our having been abandoned; the inventory of memories, how they should be presented and the meticulous attention necessary for restoring them, could help me, could help us to understand and to accept it all and to live on. And then, unlike the present which was marked by loneliness and misery and a future impossible to imagine, the past was something that actually lived. It flowed along, so to speak, it was active and knowable. *"Bullshit!"* cried Serge, pointing out both my stubborn silence as a person plagued with memories and Charlie's complicated reasonings, which were somehow not too much different from Julien's ravings. Nevertheless, our manias took the place of hope, whatever be the outcome, and God knows hope was as rare as gold during those years in that house at Grand Remous that Charles had pompously baptized: "the mansion of the departed."

That morning, then, stretched out on the old couch, while Charlie and Serge, leaving me in my ghostly trance—Serge: "Can't you see she's doing her Bernadette Soubirous act, leave her alone!"—had

65

gone off to fish in the river, and Julien was planting raspberry bushes behind the house, humming his tuneless melodies——Charles: "You don't sing, Julien, you hum like a horsefly caught in a paper bag!"—, I plunged haphazardly into the spirals of our genealogy. Or should I not say haphazardly. I didn't know it yet, but my memory, "like the memory of poets!" (Charles) was activated by my sensations. The hot sun and the itching of mosquito bites whisked me back to a July day in the distant past, humid, boiling and swarming with wasps and butterflies whose corpses were soon to be found between the pages of our papa, Georges Messier's thick dictionaries. This man, dressed in a dark suit and a wearing a white cap, was sweating heavily at the wheel of his sky blue Chevrolet and whistling *The Yellow Rose of Texas* along that sandy road going up the slope towards this immense grey house where, on our future porch, sitting up straight on our future couch with its already well worn springs, a tall very thin and very pale woman was waiting, with a thick envelop stuffed with legal papers and unpaid bills on her knees. Léa Létourneau, a sixty-four years old ruined widow, exhausted from the recent funeral of her gambling, womanizing husband. Calm and dignified beneath her lovely straw hat on that 17th of July, 1951, gently waving a fan in front of her face, she was awaiting Georges Messier, the man in the Chevrolet who had come to purchase the house, land, furniture and buildings before she set off on a road into exile that she wouldn't talk to anyone about. The fat little man, all out of breath, his suit white with dust, climbed briskly out of his car. He banged the door and doffed his hat ceremoniously, placing his foot on the porch's bottom step which began creaking under the weight of its overjoyed new owner.

Léa, grave and dignified, rose in her strangely imposing way. They gazed at one another for a good moment, neither making the slightest move. Georges was probably a bit ashamed. ("He doesn't have a pushy nature and money hasn't made him too proud!" mama was to say.) A cicada chanted, the air was boiling hot and the sky quivered as it might above a mirage.

"The house isn't haunted, you know. At least, not yet. Do come in!"

Léa gave a funny little laugh——"a laugh like a little catbird," papa would later say——before opening the slightly squeaky screen door and leading papa into the spacious sun-drenched living room. No, the house wasn't haunted at all: clean, polished, spick-and-span, the large room shone like the living room in a presbytery.

(Later, Carmen was to say, laughing: "At first, I thought your father was bringing me back to the Ursuline convent!") Three thick ferns drooped down over the pale wooden floor and the grandfather clock was ticking away, exhaling the last moments of the reign of Léa Létourneau in this huge house that made Georges' heart thump. Papa tiptoed about, still the intruder in his own castle, followed by a silent, resigned Léa, slowly and nobly taking leave of all her treasures that she offered, one by one, to this fat little man, holding out the trembling and ring-studded hand of a fallen empress.

At least, that's the way Georges would describe it to us, choosing his words delicately and, unmindful of ridicule, going so far as to imitate Léa Létourneau's elegant gestures and regal tone. In their hotel room in the village, Carmen was waiting, too embarrassed to be present, with him, at that handing over of the property and the "disgrace of a poor widow obliged to lose her home because of her scoundrel of a husband."

"My heavens, Georges, you know very well that, seeing me, the poor woman might collapse from grief and shame!"

As a matter of fact, Carmen never had any doubts about her tremendous charm, nor did she ever have any reasons to. If you were to believe her, her proud, sensual and slender figure had already made quite a few women jealous!

"A jealousy that's quite easily comprehensive, don't you think, Georges?"

(She meant "comprehensible" but Georges, always broadminded, would understand.)

"I don't want to belittle this woman when she has already been so sorely tried by fate."

Georges had ordered a cool beer and, holding Carmen on his knee well within view of all the commercial travelers having a breath of air on the hotel veranda, he carried on with his eulogy, making great gestures in describing Léa Létourneau's mansion which was also their new home.

"A large living room with eight very high windows!"

"There must be curtains?"

"Lace ones, my dear! And the armchairs! If only you saw the armchairs! as comfortable as car seats!"

"Oh, Georges, you and your cars! and bedrooms?"

"There are six, for our six children!"

"What children?"

"The ones we're going to have, of course!"

"Only with someone else are you going to have six, my dear!"

"Carmen, my sweatheart!"

"And the view?"

"Ah, Carmen, lovely hills and pink birch trees, just the kind you love, miles of pine and below, a river twisting like a good..."

"Georges, when can we go to... to our place?"

Carmen had nearly said: to Léa's place. As a matter of fact, she would never be able to forget the widow whom she had, all the same, never seen. ("It's even worse, I can just imagine her, that poor old tearful woman we chased out of her home, taking away all her memories, my Lord, it's really awful!") The ghost of Léa would be the first to come and haunt our mother's sleepless nights. But there would be even weirder ones. Books, ordered and bought by catalogue at Grolier's in Montreal would be piled along the walls of that vaunted library which would never have shelves or book cases while it would soon inflame Carmen's imagination. "It's those books," papa would say, "that are the cause of your mother's fantasies! What can you do, she has the make-up of an artist (he would never say, she is an artist), in being a night owl and cheeking people, in traveling and in her way of making life over as, as it should be! Never be ashamed of your mother, children, she's a dreamer, not a madwoman! (oh, those nasty tongues!)——, maybe even a clairvoyant, in any case, a sensitive soul, a rare bird in this world that is only too base... Love her and cherish her, as I do!" And we would nod our heads, mysteriously convinced that our mother, if she was hard to live with, was also somehow divine, she who, forever worried and sighing, was often bitter to the point of making Georges responsible for having ruined her life. (Serge: "You don't marry Scarlet, then take her to live in the backwoods!")

Three days later, Carmen and Georges, in their sky blue Chevrolet, drove back up the sandy slope towards their house with papers signed and the property paid for, as Serge was to say, "*with spot cash*", the trailer behind them filled with books, boxes and clothes, their only possessions, along with butterfly nets and that globe of the world that lit up. Suddenly, "the arrival of their lordships at the mansion" (the expression came from Charles) faded away and I closed my eyes, my head falling back upon the cushion on the couch just when Carmen was about to burst into tears in Georges' arms, on the porch looking over the pinewood and the blackish brown river that evening on the 20th of July in 1951. From that point on, I could only invent because Georges and Carmen's

68

memories diverged, for their recollections and their accounts of that night were quite different. I could claim, for example, as papa would do, that it was that first night in the house that Charlie was conceived to the sound of frogs croaking or, as mama would have it, they had both, with their eyes darting about and their hearts throbbing, spent the night listening to the hooting of an eagle owl in Léa, the widow's bed. ("My God, there was your father and I, lying in her bed like blasphemers, like usurpers!")

Our parents were fantastic allegorists. The slightest event took on all the glitter of an enigma and each memory trailed along behind it a thousand questions which kept me awake at night. So much so that, at these first evocations of the past on our couch, I began to want to push my memory even further. Already I was starting to look where I wasn't supposed to: where were they before we came along, before Grand Remous? Who were these self-imposed orphans, our parents, Georges and Carmen Messier? Their past seized my present by the tail and its secrets left the same bitter taste under my tongue and dug away the same hollow spaces beneath my footsteps as did their flight. If I were to know, I had to know it all!

I wanted to write to uncle Louis-Paul but, besides the fact that I probably wouldn't have learned a great deal (according to papa, the man had always been an *outsider* type of the worst sort), I was afraid of seeing him land at Grand Remous and load all four of us, poor orphans that we were, in the back of his truck and take us back with him to Albany, USA. So I began searching through all the papers and books in the library. That's where Charlie surprised me one evening with a map unfolded beneath my elbows and papa's strong box wide open, brimming with old lecture notes, bills from entomologists, receipts from Grolier's, pages from Eaton's catalogues, the photographs of summer dresses of every colour and of lace underwear. Then, without saying a word, my big brother stretched out, lying with his stomach on the map beside me, staring at me with a gaze that was half imploring, half inquisitive. Still silent, he began opening envelops quite gently, as though he feared seeing the smoke of some evil spirit rising from these papers with their tobacco smells. So he began reading and rummaging about, frowning, his face, however, suddenly strangely calm and untroubled. Thus was born our complicity as Nosy Parkers, our connivance at fanatical investigations that stood for us as a sort of hope. This was to go on for years. First of all, in the library, in secret, then often at night. Then, our growing craze losing all sense of proportion, we began spreading our books and maps about in the middle of the living room carpet, while Serge tried to discourage this, chastising us with his

70

cool remarks, as did Julien who was losing his "little children lost in the forest," as he liked to call all three of us. Only, Charles and I didn't look for the same things or, should I say, didn't look in the same direction. He wanted to know where our parents could have gone when they left us, to what country, to what region and to do what. Myself, I wanted to know where they came from and what they had been before we arrived on the scene. I wanted to know the whys and wherefores of this exile at Grand Remous. And then, day by day, our obsessions, which with time became more and more alike, finally came together: the explorations of the one and the diggings of the other which were most often insignificant and, above all, fruitless, brought brother and sister closer and closer together. Our nightly efforts were stirred to a fever pitch by these hopes concocted by both of us. Those years, our memories became so filled with cities and dates, landscapes and travels, words and phrases and, with the help of certain books, dreams and beliefs, that it's not astonishing that Charles became a film maker and I, a maker of trips. Our search, once set in motion, could never come to a stop, in other words, for me, it would never be satisfied by some destination that had been reached, while, for Charlie, never by some exposed fantasy. Launched as we were in pursuit of our parents, we were at one and the same time launched towards life itself, that is to say, ready to do anything so that we might learn or know or understand. As Serge was to say, much later, when he had become an easy going American: *"You would never take no or nowhere for an answer!"* Yes, ready for anything, even to save Julien in spite of himself. But that's another story, or better still, the story of another quest, another exile.

And then, when Charlie would become too obsessive, when his phobias would get all muddled up with my own, I would return to the total silence of a girl haunted with memories on my couch, my silence as a "Carmelite-traveling-through-time" (Charlie). Yes, I would return to the cloister of my recollections where a little light was burning similar to the one we took to search for Julien in the pinewood, its flame ceaselessly flickering between here and over there, between yesterday and today...

71

Aline, wherever you are, you will hear me, you too will hear me! Your yellow sunflowers taste of saffron, yes, once in a while I lick them like candies!——, this powder that you mix with your paint and that you send me to fetch at Madam Plourde's place in the village certain mornings when you're feeling inspired and when, out on the gallery, you start breathing heavily in and out like a swimmer as you peer towards the horizon. At that hour, already you're rather nostalgic, while feelings of guilt are still subdued. You leave your bed at the first light of day, go down to the kitchen and gulp down a dish of strawberries without removing their stems, and a big bowl of black instant coffee—each time I think you're drinking that varnish you used to coat your first sculpture with, the one you finally threw in the fire, the birds carved in that lovely driftwood, the odour is so similar——, and astride your rubber boots, you scurry downstairs with your old school bag that you intend to fill with cold shiny clay. I let you get as far as the pines, then I follow with my heart beating away and my pockets stuffed with strawberries. The meadowlark twitters among the ferns and the river looks like a long golden bar among the still branches. There's a smell of moist sand, hares' dung and pine gum... The sky is continually changing, passing from mauve to pink, forming bears and clusters of fruit, horses and boats above the foliage, dew drops become pearls on the velvety hawkweed stems. I crawl beneath the curved trunks of elms that are starting to die that summer, to fall as though struck by lightning, killed by that poisoned moss that I tear off their bark, my nails stained with green from this destructive jelly. My belly brushes against the knotty roots of pines down along the sand and I imagine snakes smoothed out as my weight crushes them. I slide along over the pine needles, feeling like a sturgeon working its way through the channel's lower depths. As for you, you're already paddling about in the sludge: I can hear the glug-glug of your boots along the shore then I climb onto a small mound to watch the grey underwater cloud moving in the clay around your small form which is haloed with a golden glow of light like those of the saints and martyrs in your catechism. (Where is God? God is everywhere.) And I laugh like a fool and so does Serge replying: "Not in my shorts, not in my shorts!" I slither along and coil up like a snake in a hollow between two dunes, letting nothing show but my head. With my eyes and my breath flush with the sand, I observe you. I watch you unconsciously obeying your passion for dawn and clay and I know (by this I mean, I know in your stead) that you are happy on you knees in the cool silt, with your hair in the wind, possessed by this world, receiving life and shining rays and reflecting them until you yourself become sun, river and the gleaming

72

paste of clay. And then I experience such a strong joy that I'm shaken with spasms in my nest of sand and ants. I'm your joy, Aline, I'm that slimy clay between your fingers, on your thighs, those sharp flashes of sunlight on your shoulders, that taste of seaweed on your tongue, that water as thick as oil on your belly, around your hips, its currents warmed by your passion for searching and also the song of the pines... Even though I've already begun to wish for the earth to grow smaller and for you to stop getting bigger, you above all, the ogre leaves me in peace, I'm still not buggered up either for you or for my own self. I believe each day I'm moving closer to God than are those riders of rockets in your magazines, with neither fright nor a space suit, as naked and happy as a worm in its maple-flavoured humus among the roots at our Grand Remous.

Yes, Aline, I'm spying on you. I've a great desire to see you and know you feel, at last, a little more triumphant down on the beach, I want to surprise you putting all reasoning aside and forgetting yourself, silently letting the inoffensive waves lap against your body. Later then, within an hour, all set up on the gallery where you've made it your permanent abode, between the old couch and the table with its sun-flowers, once again you'll become that tall troubled girl, with that sullen discontented face and that stiff unyielding body, deprived of her delight with clay, struggling with it all in the shadows, winning her dream inch by inch then losing it in turn, inch by inch... I sit on the gallery's bottom step, the one that's still in the sun, and I smile your way, or should I say, I smile towards an Aline that I'm trying to revive, the one with the cool salt-stained body as it was this afternoon on the beach... From time to time, you give me a cold look, a look of hardened clay, while sweeping back an untamed lock of hair with an arm covered in muck up to the elbow, an anguished hand, a grieving hand. And I lower my eyes right away, for fear you might notice in my pupils a persistent image, the most beautiful Aline of all, secretly proud and self-assured, kneeling in the clay. I endure your sighs and the squeaking of the potter's wheel (made by Serge with the fly-wheel from the widow's sewing machine) and I wait for a girl now radiant in her beauty, with that glimmer in your eye which will tell me that you really want to be happy in spite of everything. I breathe in the odour of mint crushed by my toes at the bottom of the steps: I wait patiently for your passion to show itself once again. I, who have always thought hope pointless, keep on hoping and, having never believed in prayer, even pray, counting only on miracles in which I have had no hand; continually watching for signs myself, I show them to you breathlessly and, in the end, only succeed in frightening you. Your

73

sunflowers show only half their radiance, their black centers, crudely molded and crowded with false glittering seeds, are never finished. You fling them, thickly coated, bent and twisted, against one of the gallery's pillars and go upstairs to rejoin Charles in the book room or else you stretch out like a dead woman with plaster-like arms on that old broken down sofa. I stand there gazing at your huge sad abandoned flowers begging the wind and the light to take you back. And then, I can hear you laughing up there, Charlie and you, with your artificial laughter over books and maps. You'll never find out! Then, I go back down the trail to the pinewood. With you, I've lost, Aline, but I'll win with the forest and the fields: my cages will be full of goldfinches, my raspberry bushes will have dozens of new shoots loaded with tiny white flowers like stars, my patch of clover will be swarming and yellowy with bees and, at nightfall, I'll bring you back some of their honey. Perhaps then, seeing me in the door frame at twilight, you'll take me against you and hug me fondly, forgetful of my madness and simply happy to know I can be tender and free of my terrible desire.

Aline, you big trickster, you can scream all you like about messing up your suns just as Carmen ruins her cakes (Carmen? Who can that be?) I'm aware, all the same, that you'll come downstairs this evening with your hair tied up like a feather duster, your arms all washed and now paler than your legs in your red shorts, and suddenly quite cheerful, you'll let fly my way a: "Tomorrow morning, Julien, you'll have to go in to Madam Plourde's and get me some of that yellow powder!" I'll let out a war whoop and run out onto the gallery to hug your now dry sunflowers with a fetishistic tenderness and a feeling of voodoo triumph.

Often, in the evenings, I spend a moment rubbing my quite callous palms over the smooth petals of your sunflowers and suddenly, I see you climbing the steep steps of a pyramid or walking along the white sand of a beach which is possibly there expecting me as well. And then, I quietly begin to weep because of what I've done, of course, but also simply because of time which continues to count for you, beyond everything else, and which has never counted for me, never gone by, nor will it ever: each morning, when I make my rounds of our land, you're kneeling there in the clay at the river's edge, shimmering in a joy of golden light and each evening at sundown, you're sitting on the floor up there, with your back to the wall of books, with your head in your hands, while your sighs stir the same needles in my breast.

"Ah yes, my brothers, Aline is on the road, always *on the road!* You imagined as much, didn't you?"

Our jeep skirts the gulf of California, once known as the sea of Cortes, or Vermilion sea. Everywhere we meet the debris left by unrepentant dreamers: missions in ruin, walls of rough brick eaten away by the wind, tracks leading nowhere, bits of whitened bones, abandoned mines, broken machinery. Once upon a time, conquistadores, priests, adventurers, buccaneers and pearl fishermen and today, hippies like Donald and myself, although Donald is, vaguely speaking, a photographer for *Time-Life*. Lower California, that's where I am, my brothers, at the present moment. Last night, we slept among the prickly teasels in El Portuzuelo pass, south of the Laguna Chapala. Some of the wildest regions on earth have remained empty because they are inaccessible. I keep finding myself in one of these God-forsaken spots in the world; desolate wildernesses, deserts, fossilized limits of the universe. I still have to see Mount Sinai, the Gobi Desert and maybe Patagonia.

Donald is a good companion, not a bad lover, and above all, he's a great photographer. What's more, he's knowing and funny and he answers all my questions, even the silliest ones: I'm improving my knowledge, opening my eyes and ears. As you see, I keep on running away, making new memories for myself, I'm doing my best. Today we're making our way over a mirage-like landscape divided by rocky promontories and lone creeks. The beaches are reached by following barely visible paths through thorny brush. The sandy bed of the Arroyo Grande, all pink and ochre, awaits us down in the valley. We'll be there in an hour. Donald smiles my way, catches my arm from time to time in his ruddy, sometimes burning hot, hand and I smile back. Donald Jones (I call him Indiana and that makes him laugh) is a tall auburn-blond guy from Montana. He's thirty-two, has all his teeth, is not too handsome (he says: "That beaming cowboy on the Marlboro signs is unfortunately my brother, but perhaps you'll love me a bit just the same?") but he's inquisitive and intelligent. At each oasis, after making love and having some grub, he leaves me in peace. Then, I pick up my notebook and continue with the story, mine, ours: yes, once again, I have become Aline-Scheharazade with her old couch, doing forced labour on her memories, on recounting our beginnings.

I don't know why I've begun writing in this notebook with its red cover (Charles, about now you'd say: "your colour!"), a gift from Donald. Perhaps it's to imitate my friend who, every evening, jots down his observations, the names of birds, shells and varieties of cactuses: the pitaya, the agria or " bitter" one, the blue palms, etc. At least, I believed I was doing the same as he, I wanted to and the first evenings out, I too took note in the firelight of what I had observed along the way: a red snake racing and swallowing a darkly spotted lizard, sand swept away by the current in the canyon of the laguna Salada, with its speckled granite, encrusted with algae forming brightly coloured mosaics and I even made a crude drawing of the basin of the Virgin, seen at Guadaloupe that afternoon. But after three pages, that is, three evenings of these doodlings by a gringo reporter, other words came, the first sentences, Grand Remous, the small golden sweep of our beach near the dam, the sudden sharp reality of this first summoning of memories, and I'm off again: "Everything began that morning I walked back down from the hill..." Since then, I just can't stop. Indiana says my eyes are sparkling and my brow is smooth and shiny——he says "*You're beaming!*"—when I open the notebook (Oh, our scribblers, my brothers, with their inoffensive covers, a little fisherman, a collie dog, a glowing fire from *Gone with the Wind*, our maps, our notes, papa's letters, Serge's dreams, so many words, leads, trails, this nourishment for a fanatical memory!) And when I stop, exhausted, only half relieved and still feverish, Donald looks at me, nodding his head, pleased to see I've returned to the world, and he says: "*Happy to see you surfacing!*" —as though I'd just escaped some huge dangerous wave, like that gigantic breaker at Pié de la Cuesta in which I nearly disappeared last winter, tossed about by the undertow, my arms scratched by the coral and wing shells in the shoals. (Donald wasn't with me yet, I was alone then, living that Caribbean winter of Yaqui witchcraft, philosopher's mushrooms and Mayan magic.)

Yes, I've lived like so many of my male and female fellow-travelers, one moment religious, then, a non-believer, at certain times an epicurean, then an ascetic, once a lover, next a loner, living as a hermit, then as a "groupie," back and forth, always searching and never able to anchor myself down anywhere. I continued to wander. What else could I do? Life is decidedly a madman's pastime, so, whether we live it here or elsewhere, what does it matter? "Try to hang on to hope, to God or to hell," you used to say, Serge, "it's a bit like wanting to hold your breath: if you push it a bit too hard, you risk choking to death." You were right, I no longer wanted anything. I had long stopped looking for them. I no longer looked forward to anything. I scarcely ever thought about you. Sometimes, I could see merely a few ludicrous stiff poses. Charlie holding his forehead, or else walking, like a lost monk, on the beach. Serge, wagging his head or uttering reams of soundless laughter. Or else, Julien, opening his eyes wide in the pale twilight, standing there terribly straight in the door frame, a shock of hair hanging over his brow. And I could hear the bit ends of phrases, much as certain striking replies from an old film, "relic-replies," as Charles used to say! " Folks like me, we need 'em like fireflies in the heart of winter" (Julien), "Oh, oh, this time, it's the beginning of the end!" (Serge), or else "Have to do something, can't keep him here anymore!" (Charles again.) Sometimes, I could again see the beach, the river, the hills, the house and, on the dilapidated gallery, the old couch, but as in a dream, or should I say, as a sort of aerial view: it was so small and far away! My memory was working in fits and starts. Just as, here, the wind from the sea pushes the dunes towards the hinterland, a great gust full of murmurs from my wanderings had forced back memories, had silenced voices, had blurred images. I was as far as the San Carlos mesa ten days ago, as far as the red notebook, as far as the first words——"Everything began that morning I walked down the hill..." —what Donald calls so nicely an "accidental tourist," a bogus amnesia victim, pale as marble, a storyteller who thought she had run dry. And now, when I see Grand Remous again, the house, the gallery, the couch, and the three of you, I don't know why, the dream is so close, I'm in it, I'm there too and I'm afraid! I need Donald, his warm reddish-brown hand on my shoulder, his words of encouragement that are sometimes quite comical, sometimes quite tender. "You are such a beautiful Southern-Calfornian Grand-Remousian! Don't be afraid!" Then, I go on, a bit reassured, but still trembling.

One November evening——it was raining, the roof was leaking and Serge was attempting to seal the gaps along the ceiling in the book room with linen wadding—Charlie and I discovered the Irish sweepstakes ticket between the pages of an encyclopedia on entomology. Dated June 17, 1951, it provided an answer for all the craziness surrounding the purchase of the house, Georges' everlasting holidays in his role as gentleman farmer, Carmen's "Grace of Monaco wardrobe" (Charlie) and above all, it explained their flight. And then there was those often mentioned twenty-six thousand dollars in the *Caisse populaire* at Grand Remous! ("For the children's studies and for their future," Georges supposedly told the branch manager!) I screeched, Serge fell off his step-ladder and Charlie went as pale as a sheet. We gazed at one another for a long time like three wicked cats, not saying a word, each of us incredulously fingering the red and green cardboard ticket bearing in embossed letters studded with golden rays, the fabulous sum of two hundred thousand dollars. I stretched out quickly on the bedroom's moist floor; my head was spinning, the drumming of the rain was like some sort of beckoning, a witch doctor's tom-tom calling all the village ghosts together for a huge gruesome gathering. It was as though I was in a trance, my eyelashes flickering; I felt like I was swallowing down cooking salt and my rate of breathing rose to the point that my ribs began to ache. It was then that Serge leaned over me and asked, in a scarcely recognizable voice, if I wasn't going to be ill. I answered in my owlish voice, which was strangely unaltered, that I wanted to stay there, alone, lying on the floor. My brothers walked out. I could hear their footsteps in another world, that is to say, on the stairway going down to the kitchen. The intense memory of something had taken hold of me there on the library's cold damp floor (no time to get to the couch!). I was aware that, henceforth, it would strike whenever and wherever it wished. Once alone, I painfully managed to sit up and, with my back against a wall of books, allowed myself to spiral my way meekly down the tunnel of time.

78

First of all, I observed Carmen in her evening dress, the one with the cherries printed on "Kennedy rose" silk, standing against a huge decorated pillar. She was in a rage and she was striking the pillar with her two arms which were shining brightly in all the party lights. Suddenly, Georges appeared behind her dressed in a dinner jacket similar to the one he was wearing so proudly — here, I opened my eyes a second to check — in the photo pinned on the wall before me. But papa didn't seem to be proud at all with his open collar, his two hands jammed into the pockets of his lovely suit, his thick eyebrows frowning and a well chewed cigar between his teeth. His face was the same as the one he had that evening we often spoke of, when, after having searched for Julien the whole afternoon in the pinewood, he had come home having found not a trace (Julien's first disappearance). Behind Carmen and Georges, now seated on a large stone tile dazzled with the theatrical lighting, I could make out silhouettes, people in evening dress, chatting, gesticulating and laughing very loud, even too loud. Oh yes, I remembered, I would remember each and every detail quite pitilessly! Carmen was holding Georges by the shoulders and shaking him quite vigorously.

"Stop crying, for the love of Christ!"

"Let go of me, Carmen, you're hurting me! And don't curse, I beg you!"

"Are you a coward, Georges?"

She was angry and Georges was heartbroken. Now, they were no longer moving about——their heads were close together and their shoulders brushed in a sort of pathetic rocking motion. They were both so beautiful, so solitary, so dramatic, while, at some distance behind them, there came and went the participants of a lavish party from which they had been expelled.

The scandal had just broken, their relationship—an unsuitable alliance: "Such an eminent, brilliant professor smitten with his pupil, a crazy scheming girl from a working class area!"—, this was their love. That evening, they had wanted to defy society, the university intelligentsia (ex-priests, sly and envious judges!", so Carmen was to say later). They thought they were too strong, appearing arm in arm at the graduation ceremony, light-hearted and on top of the world

—as mama would say: "Rosemary and Gatsby." And then, right in the middle of the banquet, the evening breeze having extinguished the candles on the terrace, the lights had been turned on again and then, everyone's gaze turned in their direction, the professor and his student laughing gaily in close intimacy. It was as silent as a church around the large table. Then, his lordship, the rector exclaimed in his church loft voice: "No more of that, Georges, and, may I add, don't count on returning to the faculty in September!" And, as he looking about at the entire assembly, the saintly rector added in the same breath: "The poor man!" As if the woman, Carmen, wasn't poor, wasn't, she as well, dismissed, her face pale and grimacing, to the end of the long table under those glaring lights. The others had said nothing, "the ex-priests, sly and envious judges!" Carmen and Georges were now alone, together in sin, shame and injustice. They would walk out, would leave this "university of God-fearing, ignorant, jealous numskulls" (Carmen), this narrow backward city, would abandon their plans, their illusions and run off to live in a garden of Eden, somewhere in the country. They didn't know where yet, of course, but they'd find a place and would be happy, whatever it might take. ("Oh, I was really bound to love her, your mother, my darlings!" "But I wanted him, I wanted him——Georges Messier was going to make me happy, he had to!") Georges, an ex-doctor in biology, Carmen, an ex-would be journalist, their careers broken, their love insulted, staggering along the gravel lane towards the professor's sky blue Chevrolet that they would climb into without a word, still hugging each other and shivering on that dark May evening. The door bangs and Georges sobs, repeating over and over:

"What about money, Carmen, what about money. For the love of… what about money?"

"Georges, you're gutless!"

The Chevrolet wended its way down the mountain in a night studded with the innumerable lights of Montreal, that metropolis, that city engulfed in sparkling gold. In the bedroom, I turned my eyes towards the picture of Georges in evening dress——there was my father, smiling, happy, a master of the world, a winner and a man who was still quite naive. Now, indeed, I understood. Everything was falling into place. Georges kept asking, "What about money?" A piece of luck, the winning ticket, a miracle that had come to pass shortly after the scandal and dismissal. The date on the card——June 17, 1951——spoke for itself: there was exactly one month between the fateful graduation party at the university and the two hundred thousand dollars. And then yet another month, to the very day, before the buying of the house, Léa Letourneau's old mansion at Grand Remous.

The following days, while Serge was busy going back and forth over his calculations——"I'll be the treasurer, we need one, don't we?" Charlie and I went over the pamphlets and souvenir albums of Georges' university years with a fine tooth comb. Actually we were looking for signs, for some trace of their love, this reprehensible relationship which had brought about their banishment and exile. Reports on congresses, competitions and banquets, confused photographs of a fat and pompous bishop or of some other eminence decked out in great pomp, lording it over everyone, sitting in a well-padded armchair. September, 1941, at the conference at Lake Poulin, from left to right: Jean-Paul Bonin, Maurice Veilleux, his Eminence Émilien Frenette, Adélard Quérion, Georges Messier. There was papa, small and sullen, sitting on his chair, alone, still a bachelor, we were sure, not displaying as yet that great hearty smile, the confident smile of a man who has finally met the woman of his life. The annual meeting at Rivière-aux-rats, summer,1948, from left to right: Louis-Auguste Giroux, Lionel Dupras, his Eminence Paul-Émile Léger, Clément Fortin and Georges Messier. Though still at the other end of the line, Georges looked a little more jaunty this time, with his hand in the pocket of his light suit and, on his face, the slight hint of a somewhat revealing smile. Waving the photo under my nose, Charlie kept repeating: "There, don't you see, Carmen has entered into the picture, look at the change, Aline, just look!" And I gazed at papa's face which was now, indeed, quite different—though he was beaming,

81

it was only partially so; his lips betrayed a mere half smile and his dark glasses circled a sober left eye while the right had a rather stupefied expression—as Serge used to say, "his clever clown look." And then, finally, the table of honour at the university's closing banquet in May,1951, from left to right: Mr. and Mrs. Maurice Marquis, Mr. and Mrs. Germain Saint-Laurent, his Eminence Aristide Saint-Pierre, Paul-Émile Beaudouin, Mrs. Cécile Vinet and, at the end, Georges Messier, looking radiant, slightly tipsy, nonchalantly leaning against the back of his chair with his mouth wide open ("You could count all his teeth!" — Charles), his tuxedo collar gaping wide ("You could count all his chest hairs!" — me), his hair disheveled and his glasses on the end of his nose. Carmen was certainly present in this photo without actually being there. Charlie even believed he perceived the feathery edge of her chocolate-colored hat at the lower left side of the picture. It was the last photo, the last album and the last graduation dinner for Georges. Charlie looked shattered. We never tired of calling to mind the banquet's ending, the scandal, the grief, Carmen's rancour and Georges' suffering, our mother's screeches an papa's tears, in that sky blue Chevrolet. You cried that evening, big brother, without covering your eyes, as you used to do whenever someone surprised you giving way to tears that you said you were the only one able to explain. You kept saying: "Where are they, now, how is their love for each other, now?" You wanted to know the sequel, what happened further on, but, of course, you didn't discover a thing. You were heading in the wrong direction, just like myself. To catch up with the truth, which we never really would do, it seemed best to retrace our way back down the years that had flowed tortuously by, constantly plagued by possible lies, scenes that often amounted to nothing but evasions and amusing interludes, when they weren't merely novelistic *coups de théâtre*. (Oh, how all those books had switched my memories around!) And not a single letter from her to him, or from him to her, not a single note beginning with "my love, my darling, my beloved treasure," not a single word of love composed in their hand! So then, did I have to learn to hear all over again in order to grasp what was left unsaid? As though I hadn't always been someone who was most able at catching on to things implied, at picking up poorly articulated announcements, promises and admissions... However, nothing would be of any value at all so long as I didn't know everything about us, about Grand Remous and especially about Julien, even were it to end in heartbreak!

82

Oh, that music, my brothers, that music!

Do you remember Georges' banjo? He played it like a Cajun from the hot neighbourhood of New Orleans. His music was in his image, in the image of his soul: that is to say, both negro and white, it would rise, gay and nostalgic, carefree and buoyant, into the sky at Grand Remous, or else, it dragged and scraped along, becoming the plaint of some lost sheep, some desperate prowler depriving us of our sleep. Papa claimed to have learned to play this instrument fit for exiles all by himself. But I actually followed him one evening to a shanty at the Baskatong reservoir where he went to dupe chance comers, drink beer from a still and have a game of black-jack with the old guards at the dam. ("Those men make me both happy and sad," he'll say once to Carmen who will have been waiting for him til the small hours of the morning) The oldest of these guards-drinkers-storytellers could play the banjo admirably well, and Georges, fascinated, tried to learn how to play as well. It's because of the banjo, because of *Oh! Suzanna, don't you cry for me* and *Run softly, blue river*, his preferred melancholy airs, that Georges would leave the house, once the moon was up, get into his Chevrolet, release the hand brake and let the car coast silently down the hill, start the motor at the bend and ride as far as the dam, anxious and pleased like a lover. He learned to play very quickly and, at summer's end one August evening, he gathered us around a wood fire Serge had prepared— "My word, a real woodsman. Who's to be offered in sacrifice?!" (Charlie)—drawing a gleaming bajo from a leather case shaped like an exclamation mark which had mystified the entire household since the morning when a lanky gentleman dressed like a pallbearer had arrived with a package at the wheel of a truck bearing on its sides in Gothic script: "Do-mi-sol Mount-Laurier." Crickets were chirping in the clover field, the will-o'-the wisps were climbing, like stars shooting downward, into the oak leaves above us and, sitting crouched like Indians around the flames, we waited, Carmen, with her Spanish shawl on her shoulders and a zinnia in her hair, pale and grimacing, was watching the fire as though Georges, visibly put out for several weeks, was about to convince us all, that very evening, to leap into this savage inferno. Ceremoniously, papa sounded three cords which, to us, were both surprising and reassuring: he had struck these cords like an artist, with such ease, such simplicity, his chin held high, his magician's gaze fixed on the fire which lit him up as though in a theater. The first words of *Oh! Suzanna*, followed, sung in a hoarse raspy voice—"the voice of some negro lazy-bones" (Serge)—accompanied by resounding very rhythmic cords. We were stunned! It was as though papa's fingers were moving all by themselves, finding the notes as if by magic, running back and forth over the cords, his beaming face showing not the slightest sign of effort. Louisiana, Alabama, the Carolinas, the sad yet radiant faces of black workers clambering aboard carts filled with snowy cotton: all mama's exoticism about the old South had remained, until then, abstract and remote, despite all her endeavours, her vociferous readings of *Gone with the Wind* and Flannery O'Connor's short stories; now, finally, all that entered our hearts and brought tears to our eyes. That night, even Serge wept. With crickets in support, before the glowing embers, Georges kept playing until the moon grew pale in the sky. He went on and on drawing from that banjo laments, romances and old refrains, tunes for jigging as they actually do jig in the South, nonchalantly, while swaying their hips and holding their heads towards the stars, easily changing the rhythm, often returning to *Oh! Suzanna*, at Carmen's request; having untied her hair and, standing in the firelight wrapped in her shawl, she was wriggling about and letting go some frightful cries. ("Scarlett O'Hara, whose native tara has been taken away," Charles was to say.) Even Julien took part, howling and tossing beneath the mosquito netting on his crib that was rocking away like a little boat from the isles. We weren't aware at that time that, already there in his diapers, Julien was beginning to resemble Georges' music and his banjo and that he inherited his elation from our father: at first, secret and veiled, it then became exultant even to the point of giddiness. Julien's taste for mystery and bluff, his frightening intervals of not speaking, then, his startling outbursts of warmth, his enigmatic exclamations followed by long silences during which you could hear flies soaring over the hills, all this came from Georges and his banjo. Maybe he also inherited this fatherly need to mask his beginnings, to appear, as Charles would say, later, "eternal and guiltless," dazzling, masterful, playing superbly on his soul, as though it were an instrument that had popped mysteriously out of its case. While we were charmed, troubled or terrified listeners, keeping our anguish and our questions to ourselves and disguising with a tender smile our fears of seeing

84

these marvels turn into a drama or a tragedy, we were on Carmen's side: easily bowled over but "quickly back on our skates," as Serge would say, rapidly adapting to magic or fright, apparently filled with wonder at the slightest thing, but given quite heavily to sarcasm and mockery, repressing the effects of the shock, the horror we felt at seeing reality give way to magic, preparing tormented dreams for ourselves and maybe as well, without knowing it, a future for digging in the ground or sounding the heavens, a future as fugitives, investigators and mirage chasers.

Oh no, my brothers, emotions don't grow old! Henceforth, for me, it's as though everything had always taken place at the same time. Here I am sitting, Indian-style, beside Donald at Punta Conception, in front of a beach fire, listening to some *freak* playing a guitar, and I'm over there with you at Grand Remous with my head bent towards yours, held captive by the same music, my foot beating out the same rhythm in the sand, the same astonishment with life stirring between my ribs, the same unknown claw scratching at my heart and the same shivers running over my skin, all because of Georges' banjo, a guitar player's black hair, the sky quivering with stars that seem so close, your arms around my shoulders, Donald's hand on my thigh, the glimmering light dancing on Carmen's terrible face, on Donald's reddish shoulders, and suddenly it's the same urgency for understanding and for beginning to live, at last!

> *Oh! Suzanna*
> *don't you cry for me*
> *I'm going to Alabama*
> *My banjo on my knees...*

Bahia las Animas. We are seated in the shade of an iron wood tree and we're observing the sea through binoculars. Donald is hoping to see a school of rorquals.

On a rock, quite close, in a black evening dress, much like Georges in that photo of his last banquet, a cormorant is drying his wings in the sun. I weep and I talk, I talk without being able to stop. I tell Donald: "Yes, I saw with my own eyes the rocky inlets that indent the shores and the bays. I swam in the green waters of warm seas, crisscrossed the snowy crests of sacred mountains on my fine long hiker's legs. I've gathered and gently rolled in my palms the eggs of Arctic sterns, or those of a delicate shining blue, of guillemots and petrels. I've taken logging trains that rattled along the sides of ravines that took my breath away, taken boats that danced on the swells, on the foam of beautiful threatening oceans that cast me up on beaches where I was greeted by men and women, their skin burned by wind and sun, who taught my how to live eternity in a fleeting moment, how to take possession of my real body—eyes, mouth, feet and belly , how never to count on the return of those gods, of Georges and Carmen Messier who disappeared before me in an earthly dream." And I say over and over: "What good is all that, what good?" It's the blues of an immobile traveler, her destination now being nothing but a forgotten dream. And I think of Julien, I see Julien and I believe I can hear him too! Today, it seems clear to me that, without him, without this child who existed by himself, so different from the rest of us, without his madness, his innocence and in particular, without his unwitting generosity, a victim's generosity, it's we who would have gone mad, all three of us, but with a much more fearful form of madness than his, destroying us through suffering and suspicions, tearing us apart with violent surges of revolt and anger, suffocating, as Serge could see us, in his dream-exorcisms. Julien was our misfortune in the flesh, demanding our attention, our tenderness, inciting our mistrust, keeping us on the watch, continually arousing our curiosity, stirring in us some form of courage, making of us fathers and a mother be it ever so clumsy ("Replacement parents, what can you do, it's not wonderful but it's better than nothing, isn't it " Charles used to say), allowing us to get away from our sterile searching, and Serge, from his disturbing indifference: in brief, taming us, when, all the while, we thought we were taming him. Wild little animals, boors, simpletons, fools, that was the three of us, unconsciously displaying the cunning of torturers and the cussedness of little sadists, given our secret pain, our badly healed wounds and with our agony bereft of any glory, of any heart, of any love... Oh! my God, what is happening to me?

"Indiana, I'm frightened!"

Donald places his large hot hand on the nape of my neck and speaks to me softly of my tears, of this well that finally brims over again. I hadn't cried since that time at the clinic!——thanks to a memory I so much detested. I don't understand anything, my brothers, I'm so sad and you're so far away! Grand Remous is at the other end of the world, like that frothy furrow out there at sea, Indiana, do you see it?

"A rorqual?"

Passionate, alive and intent, he seizes his camera. And myself, touched, drugged by his warmth and his excitement, I once again pick up my Ariadne's thread, but this time in both hands; I don't move away, instead, I pull now on the thread with all my strength. As though I had to find, right away today, in the very thick of the tangle, that clear line which runs through Grand Remous.

A silver arrow slashing through the calm water: that morning, Serge was swimming across the river. We were following him in a rowboat, with Georges holding the oars, Charlie and I on the rear seat and Carmen at the prow, sitting on the front end shouting:

"Right, that's the way, my love, go on! Breathe steady, now, don't get excited! Yes, that's beautiful, my love!"

Our mother had pulled her dress up and was offering her fat paunch to the sun, the belly where you were already moving, Julien. I thought: "She's going to kill it, bending over like that. She'll crush it against the side of the boat!" Georges was sweating profusely as he pulled on the oars. You could see a puffy vein swelling at his neck. Charlie didn't dare look my way, but I knew what he was thinking: "Oh no, really, what a family of fools!" You could hear Serge gasping in the water and the sun was beating down on our heads. We never wore hats. Carmen claimed that our hair, which we never washed, protected us from the sun's burning rays. And as well, this made our locks paler, almost blond, like lovely Irish heads, little Ashley's from her famous *Gone with the Wind*. "Ashley was so much more handsome and plucky than you, Georges!" I could feel my brain growing more muddled and a fierce and boiling anger rose in my skull. Without being able to hold back any longer, I screamed at Charles, through my teeth:

"She's going to kill that child!"

Carmen turned her head towards me, radiant with excitement and fury, grasping onto her hair like some tragedian about to fall into a trance:

"Perhaps that would be the best thing, my daughter! He twists about like a snake! If you'd like to know, I'm afraid of this child! And besides, I've had enough of sleepless nights waiting for him! What's more..."

"What's more, shut up!!"

It was Georges' big voice. He had dropped the oars and was glowering at Carmen with hateful righteous eyes. Then, of course, our mother smiled—"a madonna," Charles guffawed—, tossing her tress of hair onto her back:

"Pardon me, my darlings. It's the hot sun and my jangled nerves...."

Then, turning to her son, that fish, her beloved, her champion, in the river:

"That's great, my big darling! But don't give up, keep going! You're the one who'll make amends for Scarlett Messier's trampled honour!"

It was then that Charles looked at me with those expressionless eyes, like those of a dead fish, the look he had when it was really too much, when he couldn't take any more, when the sky was falling down on us, but doing it quietly, without even touching a hair of our screaming mother. I knew Charles was wild with pain and indignation, he too convinced as I was that Carmen never wanted that child and that she was hoping to smother it in her belly. It was either Charlie or me, but one of us was about to do something: howl, pull Georges' glasses off or tear Carmen's dress. Then, our mother cried, "hysterical children," while papa, quite distressed and in an extremely loud voice, uttered some screamingly funny self-evident truth, a piece of everyday common sense, some proverb or maxim that he would ask us to reflect on in silence. But we didn't do a thing. Neither of us budged, thunderstruck and holding back till later our anger and our bitter feelings, suppressing foul language and any outburst, while Serge, with his athletic crawl, tore through the water under the blazing sun spurred on by our mother's cries of encouragement.

"Oh, my wonderful boy, you're doing fine! Only a hundred more yards and you'll touch the bank!"

Georges kept rowing away, streaming with sweat. The sun was beating down. Carmen's potbelly was shining like the hump of the shark in the stories that Charlie read me, at night, that made me tremble under the covers until I could feel the monster's tail moving under my bed. Suddenly, there was a screech and Carmen began to shout: in the river, Serge was turned on his side, lying there motionless, but neither sinking nor surfacing, nor were there any bubbles.

"Dive in, someone! Come on, dive in! You want him to drown, do you?"

We all jumped into the water——with a huge splash! like a whale would make—, except for Carmen who kept yelling, standing at the boat's front end. Georges had dragged Serge back close to the boat and Charles and I pushed him on board, while our mother was pulling on his arms with all her strength.

"Oh! my love, you nearly made it! You'll be a great champion! You'll see, one day, you'll be someone!"

Serge opened his eyes almost immediately, all of a sudden, smiling and undrowned. There was laughter, shouting, hugs and the dangerous swaying of the rowboat. Then, father and his two eldest went swimming on the beach and made a long hike off along the shore while mother and her champion, lying there with his head on her fat belly, cuddled each other——two miraculous survivors. Love, great love and a day like any other, here, there was a confusion of folly, happiness, solemnity and inconsistancy: on the beach at Grand Remous, the Pumpkinhead Family, alone in the world until dusk, will forget about drownings and a future undesired birth, about life and death and words said for nothing because of the hot sun and jangled nerves.

There you are, Julien, it's perhaps because of that, their sense of the tragic and their thoughtlessness——"the mad woman and her learned slave!" (Charles)——, their casual airs and their gravity, their way of suffering and then forgetting it, their caresses and their readiness to begin all over again, while you, in Carmen's belly, you were learning terror and impatience: yes, it's perhaps because of that that you'll come and change everything, Julien, before, oh yes! well before their departure...

This evening the wind is so light it doesn't rumple the grass. For a long while, I gallop through the pinewood as a horse would do, with its hooves and its snorting, to chase away three weasels that devoured three chickens on me, last night, the savages. I take great strides and throw my arms in the air, imitating the bucking and the snapping of the whip as well: I'm telling you, a real race by a chestnut sorrel bitten by a rock snake. And I can hear your frightened laughter between the mossy pine branches. Because, you see, I can still draw out of you your nervous filly laugh. Yes, for you, words are frightening, whereas my brisk horse-like behaviour, stamping on the ferns or kneading the sand on the beach, seems natural to you: you do understand. And even if you often look at me with your great shocked eyes and your pinched mouth like a school teacher who can't get the best of the class upstart, I know that there's at least one Aline, the one I prefer, an Aline who is lively and proud of living, who is aware and well-disposed. She's the one who understands that her mad little brother is all alone, that he's atoning, paying the penalty, sitting on the verandah of that great fairy-tale house——your favorite song: "It's a mansion with long curtains in the water..." You don't know about the ogre either. You can't know since I don't say a thing (you're not the only one in the family "at times struck silent", you know!). I can't describe a presence to you, its steps, a monstrous stride that makes me lie in the grass panting as I bite my wrist and recite your poems, which I have secretly learned by heart, until the ogre retreats groaning. You would speak to me then of God or of the devil, would pronounce other words which would endow him with more wickedness and me with less courage, and that would be all. The ogre Trinité exists even if I'm the only one to know him, to crumple up in the hay or to stretch out in the creek bed, to breathe through a reed and feel the current combing my locks and changing it into woman's hair or into the hair of a drowned man, to refuse death, to prefer to turn into clay for eternity or into a long flat white rock deep below the surface rather than to let him discover me and carry me off and devour me. There you go, now I'm insane, really insane! Since I find it so blissful to be stretched out there pretending I'm dead or drowned. Watching from below the quivering of the sun and the wind, the little waves on the surface and the slow dance of the seaweed which resemble clouds in the green undulating sky. Once the ogre comes to drink as well, he's so close to my head that I can see his large eyes like those of a fly, two dead gleaming moons reflected in the stream, opening and closing very slowly like beacons. His giant mouth draws in so much water with a single lap that I can feel the   wind turn my navel and my toes to ice. I'm very afraid and at the same time, I'm crazily happy: the ogre can swallow me up so easily, I'm so tiny, scarcely as big as the snail, hanging there, stuck to the seaweed, between the monster's long teeth, still, he won't gulp me down! I'm a clear bottom of sand or of rock, absolutely motionless and smooth. I'm protected, mineralized and inedible! I breathe gently into my reed while the colossus, his thirst quenched, raises his head and the sunshine returns and makes the goldfish wriggle about my face of live stone. I half rise and remain sitting for a good while in the stream, breathing in the air like a little ogre as well before shaking myself, jumping and dancing in the sandy path, greeting the trees like someone coming back to life.

I've come to believe that you see him too. Often, you stop walking on the road to the beach and, with one hand leaning on a pine trunk and the other held like a visor against your brow, standing quite straight and on the lookout like my dog seeing a partridge, you gaze into the dark depths of the woods or at the tops of trees. Then, I approach you and murmur in your ear:

"What do you see, Aline?"

Without moving your head and in one breath, you answer:

"What do I see? Nothing really! You wouldn't understand, Julien!"

I'm sure you've noticed the immense shadow of his leg stretched out in the leaves, or heard his breathing, the snores of a sleeping monster, in the dense foliage of the sage bushes. For a minute, I'm not the only one being pursued, not the only Tom Thumb in the forest of Grand Remous. I examine alternately your gaze, the tops of trees and hollows in the underbrush and, yes, it seems to me I perceive a bit of his shaggy fur sticking out from that rock over there. Or else, I can hear him panting like a thirsty moose, down in that ravine of lilies. My fears, then, are reduced by half: you are with me, we have the same eyes that burn in our faces through straining them so hard to look at everything, our ears become such powerful antennas that the slightest stir in the pine needles makes us bend our heads or else, crouch in the wild raspberries, and then we have the same red-streaked scratches on our arms and thighs. We are accomplices on the lookout together, threatened and trembling as though we were one. And then, you get up and, laughing suddenly, let go of my hand and say in an unpleasantly clear voice:

"Poor me, I'm getting as nutty as you are, Julien!"

And you run back to Serge and Charlie along the road, leaving me there to lick my cuts, asking myself what you might have seen yourself and fearing that you are just like the others: mocking, unfair, incapable of seeing things straight and mean as well out of stubbornness and disinterest. I get back on my feet, my body as heavy as lead. I can feel my blood running as thick as oil through my veins. I attempt to run after you, but it's like running through water: I can't move, it's like I'm in quicksand. The ogre can come and get me easily, I'm paralyzed, marooned, like our rowboat when it runs aground on the sandy shoals at the mouth of the creek. I want to cry out, to shout with all my strength, but my mouth is full of mud, so I remain there on my knees in the brambles waiting for death, for the end, waiting to be devoured. You don't understand? I'm the lightening rod of Grand Remous, Aline, the ogre hunter—in appearance, I'm his prey—, I'm your healer, if you wish me to be, or even if you don't! I can foil the monster for you, ward him off, turn him away from your bodies! What you have left is your lives, your entire lives! Death can take nothing more from you, I've given and I still am giving everything for you, bit by bit! You no longer possess anything that can interest him. You can allow life to pass through you

93

like rays of light, you are as transparent as glass!

I spy on you on the beach, hidden behind a sand dune. You open your books, the atlas or one of the dusty encyclopedias from the book room where I go and search at night so as to follow your insane doings, and then, you stretch out on the sand and trot out stories of distant countries and seas: mummies, ghosts, phantoms! Why don't you run and jump in the waves? Why don't you begin to soar like that butterfly above the milkweed? You have as much, if not more, power than it has! You can do anything, you have neither weak points nor scent, you are no longer targeted, you can live your innocent passions, since I am here, for you, terrified, isolated and exposed, an attractive easy take, a prey quickly come upon, a real whipping boy, sacrificial! But you don't want this. You're not in this world yet or already you've left it, I really don't know. It's horrible: my sacrifice doesn't make you any happier, nor even more alive! On the contrary, you prefer studying, searching through books and also in your heads and your memories! And if you squabble sometimes down on the beach, suddenly exasperated, enraged by your wild imaginings, you stir up in the air clouds of ashes, not of sand, a powder that chokes me, even from afar. You don't want to recognize your good fortune: it's I who protect you from the ogre! You're in the midst of paradise and nonetheless, you're separated from it! It's you, the mad ones!

A cedar branch was scraping against the window of our bedroom through which came streams moonlight along with warm gusts from an August wind. Charlie was snoring while Serge mumbled away deliriously, the prey to one of his omen-like dreams. I wasn't sleeping myself. That night, it wasn't memories that kept your sister awake, breathing heavily under the eiderdown, with my eyes gaping at the bedroom wall on which were projected, in a shadow show, the frightening and complex entanglements of the "tree of magic spells", as Charlie called it. Doves being attacked by graceful sensual flying mares upon which grotesque dwarfs were riding or witches with mushroom hats. I closed my eyes and counted ten seconds,—when it said eleven o'clock on the dial of the alarm clock, on the dresser, lit up by the moon as though by a spotlight—during this time, panic suddenly surged up within me since I knew what was about to start jumping about on the wall if I opened my eyes. And I had to, there was no way out, so I opened them and sure enough, I began to see countries with their shifting borders, seas and continents flying about, exasperated and furious with their usual map-like immobility, their eternal frigidity as spheres and planets Australia, ploughing into a Cape Horn that was running adrift, the Berring Straits shrinking visibly, becoming tinier than our creek, then suddenly widening to let Japan through, which was nonetheless blocking this passageway by crumpling up against Norway. I made every effort to keep quiet for fear that one of my cries, or even a sigh, would cause all this geography that was dancing about on my bed to subside, allowing instead insect countries, beetles and scorpions, to swarm around on the sheets, ready to kill me at the slightest retort I might make, soundlessly, as though in reply to their mute questions: "They're in Kodiak, Alaska! No, they're at Barranquilla, in Bogota! No, at Miracatu, in Brazil! Leave me in peace, who cares where they are now, I don't want to die, go away!"

With a flourish, I pushed away the sheet which fell to the floor, a shroud, a shelter abandoned by Touaregs in the Sahara, and headed stealthily towards the rear bedroom, the one where that other lunatic lay on his little iron bed, the first, the real one, who was stricken before I was. Julien was asleep, rolled in a ball under his

95

eiderdown that I had knitted for him. The wind and the tree left no designs on his bedroom wall where the moonlight was making undulating reflections as quiet and modest as still waters. I moved, in this liquid light, towards the foot of the bed where I stopped to think a moment. Beside his bed, Julien had piled oyster shells, probably gathered along the shore at dusk. He wouldn't turn them into anything, neither a lamp nor an ashtray nor even a useless pretty sculpture, like my suns that he liked so much. These shells were simply there and there they lay, on the floor near his bed, within eye reach, within his grasp. He could look at them, touch them, run his fingers over their cold mother-of-pear, have them click in the palms of his hands like castanets and listen to the river in their funneled curves. Then, one morning, he'd throw them out the window just to hear the lovely sound they'd make bursting against a cedar trunk, quite pleased with this display of childish temper and relieved, free now to pick up plover eggs or strew pine needles on the bedroom floor to feel the prickling under his feet in the morning, or just to sleep on, to show us, at breakfast, in his impish magical way, the star-shaped traces on the skin of his back.

"At last, I'm turning into a zebra, look, a zebra!"

And we would laugh, even if we were afraid, afraid of him and afraid he might actually become a zebra, for with him anything was possible. We were especially afraid that he might never become like us: normal, terrified, rational and abandoned. On the shelf, there was a single book: Perrault's *Tales*. The night before, I had read him the two tales again. He requested them every evening that summer. He would settle himself down comfortably in his bed and listen, opening wide his great cat's eyes. Only *Tom Thumb* and The *Sleeping Beauty* interested him. He would interrupt me at every turn to ask his funny questions:

"The house in the forest where the queen ogress has her little children locked away, is it the ogre's house, the same one, Trinité the giant's cabin?"

"Perhaps.."

"The prince in *The Sleeping Beauty in the Wood* is Tom grown up, isn't he?"

"That's possible, Julien! Let me go on!"

"The two stories are really one and the same story, aren't they?"

"If you like!"

"It's a true story, eh, Aline? Are you really sure it's a true

96

story?"

I was so happy he was listening to me and talking with me and that he at last seemed alert and curious like a normal little boy! I didn't tell him that the two tales were pure fabrications. He would recite, at the same time as I, certain passages he now knew by heart, with a strangely flat voice :

"Alas, my poor children where have you come? Are you indeed aware that this is the house of an ogre who eats little children?"

Or further on:

"Is that you, my prince? You've been a long time coming!"

And then:

"He walked towards the castle that he could see at the end of a large avenue, he entered it and was a little surprised to see that none of these people had been able to follow him, because the trees had come close together as soon as he had passed..."

But, what's happening?... Memory strikes, as it has done before and oh! Julien, I don't know why, but now it's your birth I'm reliving! How far will I go backwards in time? First of all, there was the odour, the aroma of your coming into the world! I had been watching, since dawn, since Carmen's first groans—tiny cries, followed by cooing, and then something like the roar of a frightened cow—, and I was crouched behind the huge plant in the hallway. The door was partly open and I could make out four legs: those of the doctor bustling about and Georges' standing there petrified behind the corner of a rumpled sheet. But, more than anything, there was that odour, unforgettable, enough to make you reel! How could I describe, relate that sweetish discharge, half vanilla, half hen's blood, the essence of fern sap and foul sweat, like my own sweat when I would touch myself and shiver, mouth and nostrils gaping wide, during certain nights of torpour, deep satisfaction and incomprehension, deep down in my bed? The exhalations of a seashore in spring, a pure, unidentifiable, yet precise fragrance containing everything that was both desirable and poisonous in the world, the sweet pollen of murderous flowers, the freshness of a mermaid's flesh, the fetid skin of a snake, the mucus of kisses, a dying man's saliva, a drug, a potion, an irresistible appeal for a delicious death, an invitation to live... My heart was beating so fast and I was panting so hard that my breath was making a large amaranth leaf flutter under my nose like a pennant at a country fair. There were Carmen's cries and Georges' interjections that were meant to be

97

reassuring—— "Don't push so hard, my dear! Watch your breathing! That's it, my big girl, that's it!" —and the curt monotonous orders of the doctor: all these voices, and even the noises, went on *beneath* that smell, they were all fused together within that extraordinary dank odour of your birth, Julien. However, I could hear——later, with Charlie, I was to recall all this word for word, so to speak——, Carmen's wild ravings, like a witch in her frenzy and snarling with pain, along with Georges' soothing words, but which were somehow like a recording, stale, belonging to another world, a world which wasn't this odour that was the one thing capable of bringing you into life, it was both a toxic venom and a blissful balm, it was a stench from limbo. Down in my corner, I was breathing really hard, trembling and swooning, even though I remained quite awake all the while. I was listening to mama's screams and praying for her and for the child while at the same time making my own act of contrition. Carmen howled:

"Ahhh!!! What is it, Georges, what 's this monster? It's a boy, I'm sure, a tyrant! Oh, that tuft of red hair, he'll be a shrewd one one day, quite cunning! Oh, Georges...!

Finally, you came bursting out, along with that smell, Julien, within that smell, a frog in a friendly sludge, a butterfly in pollen glue! You were being born, Julien, and I was there, and I had smelt everything, breathed everything, seen it all without seeing anything, heard it all without hearing a thing! I was there, feeling drunken, sated, nauseated and exhausted at breathing in, without being able to stop, to die or to move, the aroma of your arrival, an event that would change everything, I knew it and I stayed there, panic-stricken behind the amaranth which was now quite disheveled with my fingers..

An hour later, you were in Georges' arms, red and still mute not a cry, not a gurgle, nothing. We scarcely touched you, fussing over you delicately, shyly, reverently and with a strange caution, not daring to pick you up, suddenly disquieted and liturgical, "as though a little Jesus had been born to us in the mansion" (Charlie). Your reddish down, like a tuft of fur. Your little hands: open flowers. Your dark blue eyes: two cool crystals that could already see everything without knowing what it was. Serge, his eyebrows like circumflex accents and with the toneless voice he used to relate his dreams, suddenly cried:

"He doesn't look like anyone!"

And it was true. He was neither like Georges nor Carmen nor

98

any of the three of us. A fat baby with a milky white body and hair the colour of rusty moss, already dreamy and taciturn, as silent as the world he had come from and, with each of his quiet graceful movements, he seemed to be both pointing us out and erasing our image at one and the same time. A goblin, a gnome, an elf. The imagery, the words of our tales were at last of use: we finally had him with us, the Little Prince, Rick with the Tuft or Peter Pan, Tom Thumb, this tiny god or devil who had come to us, preceded by his bewitching perfume.

I had flopped on my couch. Charles was combing through the encyclopedia, stopping at the word "heredity." (Any accident affecting the chromosomes or genes, for example, through X-rays, produces mutations...") I seized Charles by the neck. We started fighting on the staircase and I kept shouting:

"No, no, not a mutant!"

Serge pried us apart:

"Stop, the two of you! They'll hear you!"

But Carmen and Georges couldn't hear us. Locked away in their bedroom with the little mutant or little weakling, Julien, they were warbling devotedly, billing and cooing in their excitement and lisping joyfully in a tender silly baby language; in brief, they were reacting like quite normal "exhausted but delighted" parents do, (Charlie).

At bottom, we knew, of course, that Julien was our brother—"same blood, same torment!" (Serge). It was simply the fact that, with a kind of instinct which was both exciting and frightening, we could foresee both misfortune and danger: we were already preparing ourselves for survival, as though your birth, Julien, was the beginning of the end. Julien, our black sheep, our fine little madman, our martyr, our scar left with sorrow!

I'm here at Puerta Santa Catarina and the moon is setting. In my sleeping bag, no more insects, no more countries, no more teeming islands. Alone, warm and as radiant as a glowing ember, but that odour is still in the offing. It has never completely deserted me. And presently, if I rejoin Donald in his sleeping bag, I know that the odour will be there too, heady, regenerating—like a drug—I know I'll be reborn with it, in order to go on, to move a bit further along the way, so that I may finally understand the mystery of Grand Remous.

99

Returning to the barn, I find this note on the picnic table under a quartz stone as translucid and luminous as maple toffee:

> *Julien, you've killed your ogre and I've killed mine. The one that held me prisoner. You are marred with scrapes and fears as I am, but you're not dangerous!*
> *Now, I know everything,* Tom Thumb, The Sleeping Beauty in the Wood, *the mansion, the dam, the "hundred years of sleep" at Grand Remous, the doctors and death at your heels. Don't be afraid, Julien, I'm here. Together we will redeem ourselves. The ogre's lodge will become a cradle, you'll see. Have no fear. I love you and I'm waiting.*
>
> *Irene*

I raise my head. The skies are spotted with galaxies and the wind has already fallen. My brothers and my sister, she's waiting for me, the Sleeping Beauty in the wood !

A misty morning in March, the snow is melting and when it falls from the roof in clumps, it sounds like an avalanche. The words resound through me, echoing over and over, giving me the shivers: "genealogy, genealogical tree, genealogy...". I've consulted dictionaries, learned definitions by heart and now I'm trembling at the idea that I'm about to move, to finally put words to use and learn something at last! Only I can do it. (But it won't be easy!) Boom! another chunk of snow tumbles from the roof and Charlie jumps beside me. I won't tell him anything, not at least until I return in triumph from the notary, Mr. Poulin, with names and dates. I'm the one the manager of the *Caisse populaire*—our executor, if you like—has named responsible for our expenses at the mansion. As papa used to say: "Your sister has a head on her shoulders, why don't you try to act the same, you fellows!" So then, first of all, I'll go to the office tomorrow morning and find Mr. Théorêt; I'll walk down there so as to think things over, find the appropriate tone, not in any way imploring now, just reasonable, big girl. Then, I'll learn something! There's a trail, a vein, a seam leading somewhere: I knew it! And I'll follow it to the very end! I open the window to let the moist air of this first spring morning pick me up a bit. I fill my lungs with the mist that's slightly scented with tree sap and already feel delivered: I'm happy, bubbling with hope, on the war path...

Oh! how well I remember that morning of anticipation and great excitement, in the book room with Charlie, sitting on the floor beside me with his suspicious little eyes and the sudden rapidly eclipsed shadows the snow made sliding from the roof. My breath was coming in short quick gasps and my legs had pins and needles in them. I was sure of what I was doing and quite determined; it was bound to work, I was inspired, like Joan of Arc hearing her voices!

It was all quite easy. Too easy. Mr. Poulin, Grand Remous' notary, a very kind but dotty old boy, said that, for a hundred dollars, I would have my family tree. "Poor girl and those other fellows too, if you can't go forward, at least you can go the other way! And then, who knows?" ... "(Who knows what, eh, you pitiful old catholic, condescending old dope?!"——(Charlie). Mr. Théorêt didn't cause any trouble either, not that I had pleaded my case very brilliantly——"It's to pay for a leak in our roof!"——nor had he been touched by my female orphan's crocodile tears. He gave me the hundred dollars as a gift. "To pay for some silly extravagance, eh? You poor children, after all, it's just for once!" ("Oh, those 'you poor children' remarks, their understanding, the disgusting syrup of their merciful understanding!"——Charlie again). So that, finally, after a tense and uncertain eighteen day wait—considering the fact my first initiative had really been too easy—, during which springtime came, the snow melted, the ice on the river below was breaking up, and my brothers, befuddled by my interminable silences, were growing uneasy. "What's the matter with her? Usually, she gets over it in two or three days!" (Serge)——, I was summoned to the old boy, our notary's large sitting room: the tree had come! I ran out of the house "She didn't even put on her leg boots!" (Serge) and came back a little later, my heart beating, my feelings all confused, vaguely remembering the distressed face of the notary who, having accepted only half the hundred dollars, had handed me the envelop without a word and looking rather limp. Highly out of breath but basking in glory, I uttered a cry to rally everyone to the foot of the stairs, even before opening the envelop. ("You idiot! absolutely senseless!" I kept telling myself later over and over, choking back my tears, this time they were real ones, profuse and bitter.) I waited for Charlie and Serge (Julien was out fishing on the ice, playing at being a logger), seated on the couch with a large pool of melted ice at my feet. First of all, I told them about my inquiry, thereby justifying my "persistently idiotic expression" (Serge), then, on a command from Charles ("Jesus, open the damned envelop, Aline!"), with a trembling voice, I read the two pages that famous brown envelop contained. (But why, why the

102

devil didn't I go and read those horrors alone in the shed, keeping it a secret until the end, until my final disillusionment, even if it might have resulted in my lonely death?)

Blanche Rioux, born May 10,1893, at Montreal, married August 15,1910, deceased October 5, 1951.

Rodolphe Messier, born February 6, 1889, at Saint-Hubert, Married (to Blanche Rioux August 15, 1910, deceased April 12,1941.

Their children, all born in Montreal, are:
Rodrigue Messier, born June 5, 1911, deceased November 28,1948 (drown in the Lake of Two Islands),

Marie Messier, born January 27, 1912, deceased May 12, 1950 (while giving birth),

Louis-Paul Messier, born August 6, 1914, deceased at Albany, New York, December, 1960 (from an accident at work),

Georges Messier, born June 12, 1915, vanished (?) August 16, 1964, married to Carmen Dumouchel, born July 20,1924, at Chateauguay, vanished as well, August16, 1964(?).

Carmen Dumouchel, daughter of Marguerite Morssen, born September, 1894, at Charlottetown, Georgia, USA, and deceased at Chateauguay, April 18, 1964,

and of Paul-Alfred Dumouchel, born May 14, 1880 at Chateauguay, deceased October 2, 1938,

both married on May 28, 1916 at Chateauguay,

sister of Yvette Dumouchel, born July 13,1918, at Chateauguay, deceased August 7, 1945,

of Paul Dumouchel, born February 21,1920, at Chateauguay, deceased November 17, 1958.

and of Mark Morssen (?——without doubt born a Dumouchel, he will have taken the name of his maternal ancestors), born October 18, 1951, in South Korea.

Georges and Carmen Messier are the father and mother of:

Charles Messier, born at Grand Remous, January 15, 1952,

Aline Messier, born at Grand Remous, August 24, 1953,

Serge Messier, born at Grand Remous, November 4, 1954,

and of Julien Messier, born at Grand Remous, August 31, 1959.

Declared at Grand Remous, March 25, 1967, by Mr. Maurice Poulin, notary, at the request of the above mentioned Aline Messier.

Outside of the four of us—and maybe the two who vanished ——not one survivor! A hecatomb! Auschwitz, Armenia, the Goulag! Even uncle Louis-Paul had passed on (in the jaws of one of his wolves, we later learned upon writing to the Vargas circus). Certainly, Charlottetown, the Morssens, Atlanta, *Gone with the Wind*, Ashley and Carmen's "languid blacks, snowy cotton and flounced skirt" crazes became more understandable. But that's all! There, it stopped! Unless we considered our mother's brother, of course, the enigmatic Mark Morssen (whom Carmen scarcely ever talked about), dead on the field of honour, the future hero and model in Serge's stories, of his "illusions as a great little man" (Charlie), a name quickly tossed out for us, the forsaken, to toy about with, the only prey, the only demigod, the only mystery in our "woebegone state" (Charles again).

There was no doubt about it; we were alone in the world, and now for good.

"They thought he was stupid but it was really a sign of his sweet nature. He was tiny. When he was born he was no bigger than a thumb, so they called him Tom Thumb. The poor child was the butt of all the household. He was always in the wrong. Yet he was the wisest and cleverest of all the brothers..."

My heart is beating, I'm hot, I'm cold and I'm trembling, but at the same time, a strange sense of peace envelops me. The large stenciled letters give me both goose pimples and warm my blood.

"When the father and mother saw they were busy working, they slipped away unnoticed (un-noticed, I spelt out the word over and over, and then I could see you pulling up weeds in the garden, then I could see the suddenly terrifying void behind you, the deserted house...), then hurried off (oh! yes, that's it then! Hurried off!) suddenly (suddenly, yes, at a precise moment, as though given a signal!) down a side path (I can see it, the path through the pines, just beyond the raspberry patch)..."

And so it is, with my heart in my mouth and my eyes open or closed: I see, I understand and I know what's to be done:

"Tom Thumb, who was very clever, understood his parents' decision and early in the morning wished to go outside (only wished? But why the devil didn't he go out right away, without thinking about it? It was urgent!) to search for some pebbles..."

Though it matters little, it was perhaps a little later, that he does go out to pick up some pebbles. He has to! Follow these trails, one by one, in the early morning, down to the river, find pebbles and fill his pockets. First of all, with red pebbles, white pebbles, stones flecked with gold, capable of shining in the dark(and what if they flee in the night) Later, with pine cones, acorns, dried mushrooms and, given my present demented state, the hope they will be sunflower seeds and bits of bread, oh you poor foolish child!

"At first, Tom Thumb wasn't worried because he thought he could easily find the way back by means of the bits of bread that he had scattered as he passed. But he was very surprised when he noticed the birds had eaten them..."

105

By noon, the path lay bare, devoid of any markings whatever, for my crusts of bread were devoured by the jays and magpies. All the same, I hide and watch: they come down, first shy and distrustful, large mauve jays skipping from branch to branch, flitting down to the path, then walking on the pine needles as though they were embers, then darting their beaks with long sharp thrusts and the crumbs disappear in their scarcely visible mouths. Then, the long magpies arrive, hopping forward, anxious yet greedy for my pellets of bread. I return to the house vanquished, but almost happy (crazy) over this defeat: I'll have to start over. There's no mercy in this story, yet it let's me live such a forceful life. Calm, though still in the grips of my obsession, I go back up to my room, open the large book: the ogre will soon appear! ("I can smell human flesh!") I lie down and roll myself into a ball on my bed feeling crushed and spiritless. Yet, I know what I have to do some night, perhaps this very night, take a further step, enter the ogre's house and commit the act that is required (but what exactly?) For some weeks (some months? New leaves, russet leaves, the first snow of this season out of joint), I go about rereading the story but only as far as the words: "Alas, my children (the three of you and myself, reckless Tom Thumb) it's the house of an ogre who eats children." An insurmountable obstacle, the route through is barred, a high wall that blocks my way. And so, I fall asleep feeling thoroughly crushed. Each time I wake, my feet are icy cold and I grind my teeth as though, throughout the night, I had been trying to munch on white pebbles. And then, one fine night, with the moon as an accomplice and some harmless thick snow on the windowpane, once again being overly bold and self-assured , I read:

"As soon as Tom Thumb heard the ogre snoring, he woke
up his brothers and told them to dress quickly and follow him..."

But where the devil shall I take them? It's here, the only place, there's no other world, with or without an ogre. Will the tale change us, bring death back among us, or will it drive us mad, all four of us? I'm not saying, and you go and fall asleep, after having scoured your books, I mean the other books for it's you who gave me this one, the only real one, the right one: my tales! You're sleeping peacefully while I prepare to enter the ogre's house!

"He went up to the boys' bed where they were all asleep,
except for Tom Thumb who was terrified when he felt the ogre's
hand passing over his head..."

Fear? That's hardly the word! Panic, terror, cowardliness, the desire to die, mad racing through the fields, soundless bellowing towards the empty sky, passing out repeatedly in the grass, wild dives into the river, long minutes playing the drown man, stretched out under the water in the creek. It's impossible to run away. The ogre will always know how to find me. Every morning, he yells to his wife:

"Give me my seven league boots right away, so I can go and catch them!"

I'm beaten before I start, persecuted and pursued by this magical being whom I'll never be able to outwit. Hollows in rocks, fairies' hovels, the shade of a thick ash tree, the bottom of the stream, the mud in the swamp: my retreats are mere child's play for the almighty ogre, shod in his miraculous boots. I only have to stretch out, out of breath, in the hay or on the flank of a hill and just wait, my ears straining to hear the whispering stems of wild parsnips, the murmuring wings of humming-birds, my spies and my sentinels. I'm already half dead, ready to be devoured, while the rest of you, in the house or on the shore, will surely be spared, God be praised! And then, another night, terrified but mad with curiosity:

"While his brothers were running away, Tom Thumb went up to the ogre and gently pulled off his boots (oh! so gently!) and put them on..."

I'll never bring it off! Appearing to be nowhere other than the moment when he's upon me, the ogre Trinité is the fierce gardian of his enchanted boots. Nights roaming in the woods, pacing fields teeming with gibing locusts and, beneath an impassive sky, walking along a shore swarming with restless salamanders that brush against me without coming to my aid: the ogre is nowhere to be found! He must be sleeping? Where did he disappear to after seeking me out all day all over the grounds? That hill over there beyond the sugar house, isn't that he sleeping, his huge seven league boots sitting there outlined against a sky now pale with the rising sun. No, it's really a hill, the one I know so well, with its rust-stained elms which greet me by releasing their mischievous larks and bats. I'm searching for the ogre and he for me. From the pinewood to the dam, Grand Remous is a great maze. Then, another night:

"He saw the ogre leaping from mountain top to mountain top, crossing rivers as though they were streams. Tom Thumb saw a hollow rock nearby and his brothers and himself

107

under it, peeping out (yes, it's me peeping, not you!) to see what the ogre was doing..."

    At that moment, the real hell begins. Running through the woods to Trinité's cabin and finding the ogre asleep, (Oh, what a wind storm, the sleeping monster's heavy breath!) I pull on the boots quite easily and they suit me as well as the rubber waders I found one day in the shed. Next, I steal away the ogre's big knife, dash outside and fly above the fields to that dark house, our house, the widow's place. I descend the chimney like a goblin (like some demon?) I push open their bedroom door. They're asleep ("they", "the two of them"!) together, their faces lying in the shadows of her hair, their arms stretched out over the neat, quite unruffled bedcovers. I approach the bed. The moon illuminates their eyeless faces against the white (oh how white!) pillows. Suddenly, a flash of lightning streaks across the wall of the room: this is the signal! I then raise the knife, slowly, as though ceremoniously. I have to do it. The ogre demands it! If I want to save my brothers and my sister, I must obey him, it's the price to be paid, at this endless minute in that room: raising the knife so slowly, as though held by a hand other than my own, a power operating by itself within me, then the blood on the sheets, all red, my heart is rent and there's this stitch in my side that will never go away! Then, mysteriously enough, it's over. The ogre will be pleased and he'll free us. Once again, my swift exit, the chimney, my dash across the roof, an easy jump to the ground, the path where I leave red drops that the foolish magpies will drink. There's no moon in the sky, just pitch dark night and my flight across the fields. And finally, the ogre's cabin where, wide awake, he's waiting for me and welcomes me with a guffaw, a dreadful laugh that sends me fleeing again in bare feet, minus his boots that I've abandoned in a clearing, racing on and on as far as the dam. And I awaken in turn with my mouth all dry, my head an aching void, immersed to the shoulders in the flowing water. Next, it's the arrival of the men in white, brandishing their syringes like the stingers of giant wasps, doctors, the clinic.
    I paid the price, my brothers, and I went on paying!
    Each night, the same nightmare, since that famous one at the dam!
    As for her, she knows everything, now.
    I sleep every night with her in the ogre's old cabin. Yes, now that there's this redemption, you'll come. Oh, yes! you'll come!

Letter from Aline to Charles

Cape San Lucas,
Lower California

December 18

Hello, Charlie,

Ah yes, I'm wandering about here among the granite rocks along the high crooked ridge separating the Pacific from the Gulf of California. We (I'm traveling with an American photographer I like very much and I'll tell to you about him) scaled the cliffs that you see on this card so as to photograph the rocks down along the shore (they're really beautiful, eh?) and we spent hours in a boat skipping over the waves to take shots across the surface of the water of this superb grotto that cannot be reached from land (see the snap-shot I've included).

All's well. Listen, I could, I should write you about all kinds of things. For some weeks, deep down inside, I've been feeling quite buffeted about. In all, what it comes down to is Grand Remous, Grand Remous and Grand Remous! I have a lead regarding Julien, which I'm still far from making any sense out of. Let me put it this way, I've had some "recollections" (!?) I won't go into it any more here. You see, I believe our century of amnesia is coming to a close. It's all quite a business! Is it the traveling about, the distance, time, my affection for Donald—my new *hombre*—the fascination I experience for this country, its grottos that call to mind how the world began? To put it in a nut shell, I've begun to "see" again. Oh, but don't worry, I'm in control (?!) I'll write and show you. I can also see ahead, a bit.

Charlie, I want to come home. (Oh, good heavens!) As a matter of fact, this card is to announce a visit. Probably in March or April I'll be in Montreal, at your place. I'm bringing

109

myAmerican with me. We'll go to Grand Remous together to see Julien. We have to. I can't explain, but I believe it will put us at rest (?!) Your little brother can hear us, he speaks to us and continues to send forth his messages! (This I'll explain.)

Oh! Charlie, it's all been such a strain! But maybe we have to take one more step? You're feeling punch-drunk, eh? We'll talk it all over, don't frown like that! Be patient!

You can write to me care of general delivery, at San Felipe (Lower California) where I have to return in about twelve days. And where I'll probably stay a few more weeks.

You remember our dear Zorba's words: "I'm on fire, I have to put myself out!" Well, it's a bit like that, Charlie. But, I beg you, don't get frightened! We'll have time to examine things clearly, you'll see.

A big hug,

Aline

P.S. Would you please send me Serge's address?

I can't sleep. It's the very middle of the night. In the pinewood which I crossed as though in a dream, the water hen lurking in the ferns was squealing.

The moon is round and full, just as you are, Irene. Sleep, my love. Everything will happen exactly as it must. The seasons are on my side, on our side, now. I'm not afraid !

A Winter on the Beach
(News from Serge)

Cape Cod, December 20

Greetings Charles!

There's my dreams——the celebrated scribbler with the boy fishing)—, and there's me. Keep my dreams (I've given them to you), analyze away at them, go on driving yourself crazy with your old Grand Remousian ravings and leave me alone!

And Merry Christmas, big brother!

I walk on the beach all day with my camera at my neck, like the tourist I now am. Allan wants to make an exhibit in the spring of my *winter shots*. Some figures of old ladies with their young dogs, many bigger than they are, a white goose sitting gently on our verandah between a pot of geraniums and a pile of books, multi-coloured skies, greys swept with pink, pinks flecked with mauve, white and misty ones, showers of spray with and without lighthouses, imprints in the sand, the traces of passed out holiday makers, a castle of seashells with a child's face—*"alone and beaming"*, says Allan—and the stupendous self-portraits with a gardenia: I'm standing naked with legs apart, with my head bowed, head straight on, head thrown back, etc., with a raging sea in the background. Shots of an uneventful winter here in Cape Cod, a village of troubled souls relaxing, forgetful of great anxieties, distancing themselves from memory.

There's a flowering cactus on the window ledge, our Christmas tree. Allan paints and I do the cooking—today: crab meat salad and lemon sherbet—and the cats walk on the table with their stately and grave gait, just as, years ago, you and Aline used to make your funny slalom between the encyclo-pedias lying open on the floor in the book room. I don't want to think about all that and about the three of you. I don't want to, I would rather not know. It must have snowed endlessly in the fields. Grand Remous and the old mansion must look today like that creamy glistening village on the Christmas card you sent me, Charlie, with your wishes for the New Year and a question, your one and only question that sets me on edge and makes the snow blow about, this morning, on our quiet beach. You've written: "Do you still get around to dreaming?" Dream as I once did? have nightmares? or daydream and imagine life to be different? Or might it rather mean: Do you, at times, still wish to relive them? (Nothing's ever very simple with you!)

Leave me alone, Charles! I'm not homesick, at least, not

115

in the way you think. There's the sense of some distant source of comfort, it's possibly an intense feeling, but something quite vague...but Grand Remous and your endless puzzling, your questions, our questions, our old ramblings, all that history and geography from the past, all that's finished! "The sublime orphan," —I believe the expression is yours, isn't it?—has given up searching around in the dark for some explanation that wouldn't explain anything. I am the exile who, for his own salvation, rails at everything and especially at himself, and, as he goes along, forgets his anguished nights —yes, I still do dream by getting up and gazing outside. The dunes this morning are like the rounded tips of an immense iceberg slowly melting in the sun. Charles, we live, we love and we sleep on layer upon layer of the unknown, layer upon layer of mystery and terror: it's each man's lot. *"Every goddamn human being dreams of monsters!"* Allan hurls at me from time to time, weary of my startled awakenings, cleaning his brushes and getting ready to harness his own monsters by using paint on canvas. Life is a jungle of ambiguities, my big little elder brother! Don't believe ... Oh! really no, I'm not going to waste paper and ink and strain my nerves telling you about all that again. The cats make big eyes at me "full of underwater exactitude"——I don't know what American poet wrote that about cats—and suddenly I feel a great hankering for wind and salt spray, and for that bike ride I planned when I woke up. You can't get better sitting or lying still, you have to move, to search out remedies and relief. Maybe only Julien understood this and has tried to teach us so. I beg you, Charles, *leave me alone, please!* Presently, the bent shadows of poplars on the sandy road will creep further on like lava flows. I shall navigate between them, do my own slaloming, between present and future, between the streaks in my nightmares and the child drawings of my desires. *Amen and again Merry New Year and Happy Christmas to you!*

Serge

P.S. Where is Aline? In Ceylon, Estonia, Tierra del Fuego? Do you have any news?

116

Big brother,

That's a real fast reply! Aline's in Lower California, who would have believed it? And with a man! An American as well. Would it be, in both our cases, the ghost of our handsome heroic uncle Morssen welling up again? ("It's just not possible, not possible!") I'm stunned, but actually not too surprised. Our sister is an adventurer and a "late bloomer", we knew that, didn't we? And a "muddler and a trouble-maker!" as papa used to say when he grew weary of all our questions.

If I've understood correctly, Aline has a new plan? I'm on my guard, I'm scared and fear the worst! My unconscious that's "collective" as everyone knows——rebels, bucks and grows quite unruly, that is to say, it gets on Allan's nerves for he's taken the train for New York and left me alone with my *family bits and pieces*. Suffering can so easily end up being ridiculous, don't you think, Charles? I talk to the cats who shiver and stare at me as though I was from the SPCA, I pedal down the hillsides and, this morning, I forgot to turn out the lamp in my dark bedroom. The result: some rather frightful skies with flights of vulture-like gulls and hellish black mist. With me too, something is going on (?!). It's very vague, very unpleasant and probably totally meaningless, once again. But all the same, I feel... a small upheaval, a shivering and I often have what my dear Allan calls an *"omen-stricken look."* After you, who actually wished for your destiny as a scourer of ruins, will Aline and I, in turn, late in the day, become artists (*my God!*)? There's still your (our?) touch of madness, isn't there? At bottom, our differences are quite similar, don't you think? "Severe ailments require drastic remedies," you write. That's very clever, but what do you mean by "drastic remedies"? It seems to me we've really

117

given it our best try, we've taken every train and plane, reread *Gone with the Wind* twenty times, sometimes even confusing Carmen and Scarlett, we questioned Julien's doctors, we even tried forgetting: and all this led to absolutely nothing, right? What a muddle! What a *mumbo-jumbo*! And suddenly our sister, from the other end of the world, inspired once again——Lord Jesus,——whether by the unexpected affection of her last *boy friend*, or by the astounding memory of either one or the other of her "splendid Mayas" or, as you write, by gazing at some "womb-like grotto" (wow!), wants to start up again? And you want me to "cooperate"? *What a zoo story, brother!* She's on another scent, you say? Aren't you scared hearing that? And Julien? Do you think he's changed? Do you believe, as I do, he can hear us, see us?

Wait now, something comes back quite vividly: Once, I went hunting with him, at the back of our land. Aline and you were locked away again that day in the book room. (You had some lead or other!) We hurried through the pines, Julien was in a very good mood: his traps were full of hares. The forest was aflame with blood red leaves, mauve leaves and silvery ones, and the sky was a startling blue. I wanted to talk to Julien, put him on guard——Jesus, I don't know what I wanted to tell him——, I was trying to get close to him. I could feel he was distraught: it was on one of our rescue visits, a few weeks before he went to the clinic. As soon as I tried to mumble something, Julien made me stop, putting his big hand that smelled of blood on my mouth. He kept saying:

"Shut up ! The partridges will hear you!"

Then, he smiled, with his heart-rending crazy smile. He didn't want to hear me. I would have liked to shout:

"You're not crazy, Julien, you're doing it on purpose! Tell me why! Tell me what's the matter!"

I couldn't get through. I didn't say a thing. But I'm sure he heard my questions. He knew that I knew that he knew, etc. While the eye under that perpetual reddish shock of hair was scarcely a glimmer, his deranged green one seemed to be saying to me: "Everything will go along much better if we don't let words get in the way," or something to that effect. Suddenly, a partridge flew among the branches right in front of us with a funny noise—do you remember? Julien scraped a bit of cardboard with his fingernail, close to our ears, and we saw the bird fly up—and I fired. The little creature fell with a thud onto a carpet of pine needles. Then, Julien looked at me and said with a straight face:

"Do you want me to show you where they are?"

"They? Who's 'they', Julien?"

He looked at me without flinching. What was he trying to tell me, and why this fearful look? I was afraid and ran home, scraping my shins on the thorn bushes.

Wasn't that *terrifying*,——Charlie?

Go back to Grand Remous? My goodness! I don't know, really I don't. I'm going to stroll on the beach and try to think it over(?!). Give my address all the same to our Lower-Californian visionary today, Brazilian lady tomorrow and... *What the hell*, we'll see! But don't count on any volcanic awakening, eh? For me, *the voices are long dead.*

So long, elder brother and give me a bit of time, OK?

Sergio

119

Cape Cod, Mass., February 6

Greetings, big elder ninny!

I shouldn't have phoned you, here I am, all topsy-turvy!

Surely, the best way of transforming a dream (which may be liberating) into a nightmare is to tell you about it on the phone! In writing this letter, I would like to try to " untangle the threads," as we used to say.

First of all, I thought I told you (or wrote) that I too had gone to Georgia and Virginia and that I had seen Carmen kneeling in a park. Of course, it wasn't actually her, but I got a shock, perhaps even the fright of my life. Still today, I sometimes think that, if I'd been able to overcome my qualms, if I'd talked to that woman—a hippie praying? A tramp? A pure and simple apparition?—maybe I would have understood something and maybe, I would have had a "real conversation" with my mother. Drop it, you wouldn't understand it, Charlie. Let's turn to other things. Let us merely remember the fact that the event had made such a strong impression on me, that this woman, the Carmen of Richmond, kept reappearing night after night in my dreams. Of course, each time, she spoke to me and I to her. It was and it wasn't our mother. *For God's sake*, Charlie, I'm not going to start lecturing you here on the hazy nature of dreams. You know how they work, don't you? Even if I'm the one you named the "number one great dreamer" in the family, it must occasionally happen for you to spend a brief moment of some anxious night not knowing who you are, where you are, and who these human ghosts are waving at you while appearing so close and yet so far away. *Give me a break!* Is it really conceivable that I've deprived you of your dreams by speaking so lavishly about my own? *Grow up!*, as they say here. All right, there we go! The dream has come back. Richmond, the park, the dew on the grass, the halo around the woman, my apprehension, my meek shadowy steps towards her, etc. Except that, now it's always the dress of that woman, Carmen, but the back of it, the nave and Julien's reddish blond braids that I perceive, while moving towards this vision. That's all. Never do I reach her, or him (?!) My gaze is suddenly (in the dream, Charlie, Jesus!) drawn to a fountain splashing a little further on, or by the disorderly takeoff of a flock of pigeons. And then, as though a video tape were slipped into my machine, my brain begins playing back all kinds of images of that trip which, aside from that apparition and certainly because of it, have disappeared from my mind. Red brick walls crawling with vines, a university football field where some huge very handsome and half-naked guys are tossing a tiny ball around, a roadway of yellowy sand and some fields of almost an emerald green that slowly, almost harmoniously, slip by as though I were on horseback or on a bicycle, and not in a bus. And then, all broken up, certain anachronistic, hallucinatory scenes from *Gone with the Wind*, read and seen over and over to the point of nausea, you can well surmise. I also often see uncle Mark, blond, merry and wonderful, standing there quite straight in his soldier's tunic. Why? In these dreams, he has Carmen's sad smile. He's like a sentinel or a policeman who's come for one of us (?!)

All right, that's enough, it's all gone with the wind and long ago, isn't that so? Before you begin worrying and send me a kindly therapist, "love-assistance" style——you're such a big elder ninny!——, I'll close this wailing letter with a hug, begging you once again to only half count, only a third, what am I saying?, only count a quarter on my springtime visit for that great reunion Aline has orchestrated (though she still hasn't written me!) *We'll see in time!* And what about that dream? Have you caught on, will you manage to analyze it all? (*Bullshit!*)

> *Peace and love,*
> *Serge, the dream speaker*

P.S. Could you make a taping of your film starring Julien, Grand Remous in person (do you remember?), and send it to me? *Thanx !*

121

Little Aline (the Great)

I have difficulty believing this letter will find you in your "valley with a wide sandy bed called the Arroyo Grande." I'd really like to see and breathe in your brittle-bushes, your great mescal producing agaves, and your "small decorative mescalillos," and also, sitting there in the sun, extract my boot heals from the prickly pears. Dear Aline, just as in times gone by, you make words sing and make me long to go and see the world and, at the same time, instill in me the fear of getting lost in it. I'm living, here, at the foot of some very peaceful old sand dunes, by a fairly inoffensive sea, beneath some large protective trees. Prema-turely retired, uninvolved, withdrawn, *as you like it*. I stretch out in my hammock and listen to a lawnmower droning, as I leaf through *The Tour of the World in Eighty Days*. I find this exotic. I sit near the window, gaze out at the little deserted beach and the great stormy winter sea, drink a cup of coffee, listen to a Mozart recording, then get up, suddenly troubled continually flooding over, as you know?——and go for a long run on the boardwalk. I also take heaps of photos, to believe all this, make it exist, this *winter paradise*, the dunes, the huge waves, the trees, but also my life, which never could——or wanted to really become fixed to anything——*Same old story!*

I stop short——like Julien's dog might before a hare gazing at this photo you sent me of yourself. Allan—Charlie, our go-between, must have told you about my American? tells me you're *a stunning beauty*! I agree entirely, but I'm struck by the fact that today you are Carmen's age, when she took the keys to freedom (leaving poor you the keys to the house!) You don't look like her at all, if just perhaps a very little bit in the way you slope and sway which is more Mediterranean than Grand Remousian. However, just to see you like that, haughty, thirty-nine years old, with all your teeth and as dark as dark, I start imagining our mother (quite involuntarily, but are you aware just how crafty my "collective unconscious is"?) still "young and ecstatic" (the expression is probably Charlie's) clambering up cliffs or diving into the emerald swirl (while Georges, holding forth a butterfly net, combs the brittlebushes with that eternal burnt out cigar in his teeth, of course!) It really doesn't hurt any more, but it hurts a little just the same, doesn't it? Imagining them alive, still young, happy and, above all, other, different? That should spur us on, drive us, fire us up, shouldn't it(?!) I really don't know! However, it makes no difference at all, and we sit there panic-stricken and paralyzed—at least I do, in any case, except when I go for a run and also, periodically, when I feel desire, with Allan and sometimes, rarely with others——noticing that nothing ever really happens, despite the insanity and pigheadedness of these "people heady with sources," other well or badly raised children but raised just the same, the "normal" ones who hurl themselves headlong into ludicrous suicidal adventures believing they are involved in meaningful endeavors (*money, sex and war!*). My Lord, do you remember Charlie's graduation photo, how funny and terrible it was? Eyes half closed, as though about to die, a living corpse, and under the portrait in Gothic script his ridiculous motto "To live, to live!" All right then, that's just what I'm talking about: our desire to cut free, Aline, and our sluggishness.

There you are. With all this, I'm beginning to feel a bit more despondent, but a lot less puzzled than I really am. This is what makes me both modern and ridiculous, but perhaps rather clearheaded as well. And as one of your poet friends has written——I've managed to retain some of them, just the same, and, better still, I do a bit of reading now! "Lucidity is the wound which is closest the sun." Yes, indeed, when in life, you've really no mold, then you can only find your place in culture, in record performances, in others or in the love or the fear of others. Myself, I've always sought tenderness in some overly strong person's arms like those women today who are said to "love too much." (?) As for Julien, he's paid quite dearly for his lack of culture, his wildness and his loneliness, but perhaps this is the price of

123

innocence (or of insanity?). (I'll tell you something later about *Julien the Magificent*). You may skip some passages of this epistle—I know you're yearning to know about the *spring-call* at Grand Remous—but words, each and every one of them, do me good. For years now I've been bustling about, running, moving here and there, fleeing or catching up to myself, in silence, always silent and moving, as though one of your Lower-Californian snakes was brushing against my thigh and making me continually skidoo. Oh, I never go very far! I cross the street and go into a gym—I still break records, win games sometimes—or I go to a café—I drink only juice, of course, still terribly afraid of alcohol!, or else I return to the beach, threading my way here and there among the dunes, being pursued or pursuing what? I let my heart slow, caress my neck and my brow and repeat over and over: "You're lucky, you're alive! There's so many who die!" (Surely, you know what I'm talking about?) The Earth is badly wasted, our dreams, distorted and distressing, now take place on television, adventure is dead and science, which is supposedly all-powerful, still can't find the vaccine! But, it's true, I'm alive and I've a lot to tell. Often, I'd like to scream, but I merely blow seaward as I gaze at the horizon. I should be either superhappy or suicidal, the one or the other and nothing else. But it's as though I am on suspended sentence between an apocalyptic past and a nuclear future, in purgatory or in limbo. Offered up as an orphan, am I still to be sacrificed, now and forever? Even if you don't play, you lose, that's the way it is. (Do you know? A new bar has just opened here that they've called: "Maximum security. That speaks for itself, doesn't it?) When I think of what you must have been saying about me: "He's letting himself live, our handsome Serge, he's taking it easy, he's chosen to forget, etc." How deaf and blind you've been (but evidently not speechless, alas!) all three of you! Or else, I've really taken you in!

Why am I writing you all this? Probably some cells on the fritz, both worn out and over stimulated, like those Boston teenagers seen landing on the beach on Sundays in summer, in luminous shirts, dragging their feet and shouting Sioux warrior cries that send the geese flying, suddenly desirous of advancing their migration north by several months. Yes, indeed, even tundra is preferable to remaining there on the sand or splashing about in the waves, trying "to find one's sense of logic in this chaos," as Charlie writes in his last overly fraternal missive.

Now then. A last attempt at a rescue? A homage? A poetic justification for all these years of guilt? Or quite simply, a work of art using our youngest brother as an excuse? *Julien the Magnificent*, Charles' last film, is one more drop of water, a fatal drop falling in the mill of this "nobly inspired deception,"as he himself writes regarding his work. You really must see it, this short lyrical documentary, "filmed in total disorder" (but how could it be otherwise?) showing us a sort of kindly hermit, like some *coureur de bois* Lanza del Vasto, story-teller and comic, just bubbling over with juicy anecdotes but avoiding the basic essentials. A return to the earth, sublime 'dawn of the world' sunrises, allegories regarding talking rivers and the four seasons, relating the fickleness of the human heart, and it goes on like that for thirty minutes (fortunately, no longer); maple syrup and magic potion all in the same vial and labeled "Grand Remous, deadly poison." In turn, I become overly angry or laugh too much as I once again scan these pictures of our brother by the creek, standing above the sluice gates, at the top of the hill or on the steps of the mansion's verandah....

I have never spoken about it, Aline, but once, about ten years ago (*God, time is so much more than money!*) I received a letter from Julien. Actually, it was more a plan of the grounds, of Grand Remous and its surroundings, a sort of scribbled drawing of the mansion, the hill, the pine forest and the dam. He had made ink sketches of us all on the mansion's gallery. Then arrows, zigzags, stars (and ink blots here and there) a kind of path leading, more or less, from the sluice gates to the mouth of the creek. And just below this, a shakily written: "Bravo there, champ, you'll find it!" (???) The envelope bore the address of the clinic at Maniwaki. Of course, I didn't reply. And then, I forgot this insane letter, until recently, that is, when the dreams started again. Every night, I go for a swim in that creek, follow the current down to the little bay, get trapped in the swirling waters just above the dam; then I wake up, feeling as though I'm suffocating. Each night, it's the same terror I knew years ago and then I get up and watch Charles' film again on the video, the creek and the rushing waters: I stop the picture and a violent trembling takes hold of me as I watch the water, the waterfall... I don't know what's come over me! I laugh and tremble at the same time. In the film, Julien is looking at us, he wants to tell us something! That scene in the cabin! His hand, quivering with anguish, points out the bottles of whisky all artistically aligned on the workbench and I can hear the old rifle shots—, "Did he kill himself, is he firing in the air? "Don't you remember?—and I'm frightened by his eyes that are gazing at the camera, then looking at us, wishing we would understand, but what exactly?

Oh! I'm not annoyed with Charles. Once again, he's shown himself to be sensitive and kind, that is to say, unconsciously and unwillingly idiotic and cruel. We've done as much ourselves and even worse (our cowardice, our own betrayal just before the clinic incident, etc.) His terrible responsibility as the eldest brother——haven't we suffered enough because of it, you and I, not to speak of Julien!——has

126

never allowed him to let go for a moment and show a bit of tenderness. However, let it be, we love him as he is, and so on. That's really not it, Aline. The real problem is that we have to constantly go back over everything—back to the scene of the crime!——and mess up our chances by confusing all our sources——God, help me here!—the fact is we are forever in an orphan state, forever abandoned children! At that point of no return, in original sin, under the sword of Damocles, anything you like, and there's no way out! It's horrible, laughable and irreversible! Neither a brotherly film, nor travels in search of some useless forms of magic, nor some ironic exile on a quiet beach will ever stamp out this thing which makes Charles, you and myself like strangers passing by, like eyes and voices in the night, like wanderers never able to cross the frontier between memory and life, and so on! In the same way a person can become a heroin addict, he can become addicted to suffering. A taste for natural living loses its fine edge, a capacity for joy degenerates and, in the end, wherever you are, you find yourself lying in a desert with a rather sickly horizon. Except, of course, if you choose (?) madness, and this brings me back once again to *Julien the Magnificent*: yes, maybe insanity, illness and alcohol are shields intended to protect man from his own collapse. Anyway, how am I supposed to know now, my great little Aline?

Indeed, this finally brings me to this stirring spring rendezvous at Grand Remous which you've invited us to so warmly, you, the hostess exiled for such a time from that mansion. *Why don't you stay where you are with your beloved photographer?* Why come back? Why try again? there's no miracle in view, Aline, come now! What are you hoping for? Or, rather, what do you really want with you story of *Tom Thumb* and *The Sleeping Beauty in the Wood*? It's totally incomprehensible!

I'm tired——yes, yes, the ghosts are back now, every night!——, depressed and deeply convinced how wild, how absurd and how completely useless all this is! I'm going for a run on my wintery beach.

Try your luck again, if you feel able and if you wish

(?!) But speak to me mainly about lagoons, canyons and azure blue beetles. In particular, speak to me of mirages, *our last and only chance, sister!*
　　With tender cool kisses,

Sergio

Cape Cod, March 16

Will be in Montreal on the 25th —— stop —— am
definitely too weak —— you wore me down —— but it's all so very
pointless —— stop —— be at central station, please! —— stop.

Serge

Grand Remous
(Julien)

I smile, from time to time, and keep saying over and over: "Tomorrow, they'll know, they'll know very soon. Be patient!" And I listen to them absentmindedly as I fill their cups with hot coffee.

Charles closes the book (yet another one!) smiling with his crooked little wolf cub smile. Oh! how alike the three of them are, sitting there all crowded together on the old couch, and how much they resemble that three-headed child monster of yesteryear, shouting with laughter, opening books, scribblers and albums, unfolding maps, sifting through the "archives" I've laid out on the table, just as I sprinkle bits of grain on stumps, every morning, to attract rare birds. And they open the books and read here and there passages they underlined in the past, which still today reawaken, as though they were new words, a sort of tender sorrow, that original sin, and make their faces shine like moon surfaces.

It's snowing. In the morning they'll know! They'll come over that way! We still have some more surprises in store for them. But they're talking away and I don't stop them. They've forgotten me, once again and probably for the last time.

All three of them nod their heads in unison. They're reading and smiling, just like angels around the crib at Christmas time. It's still snowing. Outside the living room window, the last wintry winds are gusting. But soon that will stop. Tomorrow, the already glimmering ring of bluish grass will grow larger at the base of the pines. The haw-finches will no longer be hopping along the cherry tree branches; they'll have gone further north and I'll be waiting for all three of them up there. I waxed the skis, took out the boots, hung out the overcoats that smelled of mothballs on the clothes line, and prepared the thermoses of coffee and rum that they can heat up on the stove at daylight. The American, sitting to one side, observes all four of us as though we were a herd in a paddock. I don't like his gaze which holds us in judgment.

They arrived this afternoon in Charles' old jalopy, the American with them.... Slightly merry visitors who are just passing by, of course, but who have come to fight on the great meadow along the river bank. Not to fight among themselves or even with me, but with the springtime that Grand Remous and I have prepared for them. I'm quite calm and I smile their way. The madman is gentle, the madman is free of his spell. I love them enough to split the ice on the river, enough to give my life, to *triumph over time, and I'll show them, I'll show them! The snow will be soft and heavy, the green of the pine needles oily and shiny and all the way downhill there will be the smell of sap. They'll hear the flute-like song of the ring-necked meadowlark hidden among the old bulrushes who's both disturbed and happy to be ahead of the good weather. Oh, above all, let me not spoil everything by letting my joy burst forth too soon, don't let me squander my revenge!*

I quite decidedly don't like that heavily tanned American who talks of going to see the dam. In the glow of the cherry wood fire, they all look reddish-brown and chatty, nervous and still unaware: though they are unconscious of it, they are living a kind of combat vigil. They're talking and laughing as they did in the good old days! But perhaps all three of them sense what's coming and are trying to hang on to the tactics of the past, their old tricks? It's a wasted effort; I have no wiles at my disposal, but quite clearly an art mastered patiently and passionately, which is much more powerful than the sterile magic of memories or of a doctor's drugs. An art—my revenge! my redemption!

Then, suddenly, there's a heavy silence. Charlie, perched on a step in the middle of the stairs, squints in my direction as though I were an apparition from one or the other of his intricate films. Aline, standing near the tall fern, looks at me quite openly with her large explorer's eyes. As for Serge, he's stretched out on the couch, staring about, casting sidelong glances my way, as though not wanting to show me how incredulous he feels. Naturally, it's he who says in a voice coarsened with the fatigue caused by a long trip or, for that matter, by an entire lifetime (he's evidently not aware of the fact):

"Is your outing very far, Julien?"

I don't answer. I smile, holding my gaze steadily upon his own. The American, sitting in the rocker with his hands on his knees, doesn't move a muscle.

"How's about going to bed?"

That was our big brother. Yes, they're relieved now, saying: "Good idea!" and "Good night!" along with clumsy anxious hugs and kisses in my hair; their warmth merely momentary, carefully measured, shy and polite. Then, they clamber upstairs to sleep in their rooms which I have carefully set out with fresh sheets, a bright lamp, books and maps on the dresser and bare white walls so that the shadows of the night, my accomplices, may stand out more forcibly. My sorcery is for the American as well, and why not?

Yes, I spoke of an outing, a hike, a picnic. Very soon, tomorrow,

134

*they will see. I can hear them laughing and murmuring in the bedroom
with all the books where I have, of course, restored every volume and
scribbler to its rightful place. I stay in the living room for a moment
poking the fire, smiling at the embers and savouring my good fortune.
All three of them have come together, at last! Then, I walk outside into
the darkness. Victory! It's stopped snowing! The weather obeys me like it
would a god!*

*I could reach out and touch the stars. I breathe in deeply but it's
not enough. I would need the lungs of a bear, a porpoise or a buffalo to
devour all the air of this night. Evidently, my body has always known
about this night, the springtime and what I am preparing. It's passing
quickly, oh, how quickly! Their brains have done their poisonous work at
digging up secrets, but their hearts haven't wavered: they've come!
Tomorrow they quite easily come sliding along to join us. And the
American will be with them, taking photos, and why shouldn't he?*

*I run into the pinewood. Desire and fright mingle in the forest
air. I'm a wounded deer losing its blood on the stones. I'm the one who
took away, then gave life! I'm the ogre of Grand Remous! Scarcely
marked by my slight shadow, the path winds its way through the
moonlight descending as far as the river. Grand Remous becomes the
domain of a Robinson in the moon's bluish glow! The smell of birth is
everywhere! I run faster and faster. Now, I dash through sage bushes. Up
there in that little cottage, a light is flickering among the leaves. Rapidly,
I mount the hill again, following the path that is cleared of snow, shoving
white pebbles in my pockets as I go. Will they see? Will they understand?
The tale, since it is and since it was a book, first of all their book, is
certainly not far away, they won't have forgotten! They have such
tenacious memories! Yes, they will understand and they'll come. I
scramble along, my pockets now stuffed with pebbles: I'm already within
view of their car, of the porch and the mansion. They're asleep and all the
fires are out. They're renewing their strength. They're a bit aware, that's
for sure; their attention stirs at the slightest thing. They've always been
in a state of permanent alert. They'll put on the skis that I've prepared
for them and that they'll have found on the porch, and they'll come
down the hill. Is the dawn of day still far off beyond the pines? What is
time then, at this beginning of the world? An empty spot in the wind, a
hare's breath, a river of stars that breaks its dike and rains down upon
me? The skis, their seven league boots, and this granular snow, the white
desert they have to cross, and then the springtime down below, at the
edge of the still frozen river. Up above, in the bedrooms, the dancing of*

shadows has begun its play on the walls. They are sleepless in their sleep: they glide down rumbling currents; they roll in an afterbirth of desires; presently, they will be born too, they're about to awaken from their hundred year sleep. In their bodies, something heartrending is moving, shouting, twisting, singing! They heard me and they've come! But that tall reddish brown silent fellow with the overly bright eyes, will he stay as well? If so, he too, along with the others, is about to fling himself upon the coming daylight! They'll be riddled and burned with its rays!

I slip down the porch steps taking care not to make the planks creak: I'm as light as on that terrible night years ago, a shadow in the clear night. I put on my skis and rush in one bound to the first line of pines. I immediately find myself in the pinewood's heavy darkness. What a sudden silence there is in the world. Spring is preparing itself monstrously and noiselessly beneath the snow. It's just like me. I roll three pebbles in each of my palms: a shepherd's stars for the three magi kings asleep in the house. White pebbles on the snow, yet they'll see them. They'll know that these signs can only be mine. They'll think, and maybe even say: "He's mad again, it's another attack; let's follow the stones and we'll find him dead drunk or even worse..." Making them come is what matters! Then, they'll follow my ski tracks. All the same, I scatter my pebbles quite sparingly. I perch them like round smooth birds on swells still covered with an icy coating of snow. Sometimes, I nestle a larger more shiny one, with silver and golden eyes that will sparkle in the sun, in a woodpecker's tree home, leaving it quite visible. Tom Thumb's really getting carried away——he has the right, he's waited so long! From time to time, I turn about to gaze at my ribbon of dream-world stones lying here and there on the snow and the dark mansion at the top of the hill where my sister and brothers are sleeping. I catch tiny drops of sap on the bark of willow trees and lick them down, feeling my earlier fears melt away with them beneath my tongue. It's over. I've redeemed myself and that's all my brothers will know. They'll learn nothing about this new ogre, will never ever be aware of anything, whether it be about this other one or about that night at the dam. No, never!

Arriving at the river bank where the sand is already showing through the snow, I let the last of the pebbles fall from my pocket, the tiniest ones snaking their way to the foot of the stairway of logs that leads up towards the cottage, towards the crib. I take off my skis and place them on the steps. Before going up, and so as not to smother them with my exuberance, I roll my pants up and march forward up to my thighs in the icy river. The shivers that invade me are the same as those that

136

were running through your belly, my love, my Sleeping Beauty, my revenge.

I had never driven a car and, as for trucks, it was the same thing. However, I took the wheel of your little pick-up and we raced towards the hospital at Maniwaki, taking all the side roads and short cuts, like those legendary canoe men, said to be possessed, who, in the power of the Devil, traveled across the skies. You both groaned and laughed at every hole or pot hole we'd hit along the old sandy road. The waters broke just when we were crossing the bridge and I yelled: "That's a good sign!". You smiled as you caught hold of my hand. At the hospital, they wanted you to sit in a wheelchair, but you refused and I carried you to the "labour room" as they call it. I kept talking to you and you looked at me, and I thought: "We love each other; we scarcely know each other and we're in love; we've found each other and come back again and again; we've had our revenge and now, we are three, and when they arrive, we'll be a clan, a real family, a hell of a tribe!" Right away, you had some heavy contractions. While your eyes seemed to brighten the room, the doctor shouted: "Wait there, girl, don't push!" I squeezed your arm hard, probably too hard, as though it were my job to bring that child into the world. And it never came into my mind to ask: "What if it died?" Just as he never thought: "What if I were born an orphan?" He came quite quickly, his dark head, his little frog-like body, his shoulders that hurt you——you cried out with a long hoarse wail that will echo in my ears all my life!——and then that warm little oily head was in my hands and I brought it forward; certainly, it was up to me to pull it into this world. And it wanted my hands. It slid over my palms, slipped into my arms. Then, that little fish swam onto your tummy where I lay it down gently. You slept for a minute afterwards, breathing heavily, while I bathed the little one in a basin, thinking of the river, of him and you and the river, of all three of us, then, of the six of us in the river, in the springtime and during the summer, of my redemption and of the world that was about to begin again at Grand Remous.

I sprang up the stairs four steps at a time. At the edge of the sky between the pines, there was a glimmer of daylight. You're probably asleep in the big bed, the little one lying against you. For the last time, I look towards the hills, towards the mansion where they must be waking up now, one by one, emerging from limbo and returning to the world, the American as well as the others. Is it possible Charles has even found the first stones (It will certainly be he!)?

But why, with my hand on the door knob, am I suddenly afraid? Oh! I beg you, if somebody must pay for all that's happened, let it be me and not this child!

The Dam
(Aline)

He had prepared thermoses of coffee for us in the kitchen. He wasn't to be found either in the house or in the pinewood. We weren't surprised, of course: once again he had vanished so as just to frighten us a bit. We drank our coffee without saying a word. All four of us sat around the table in a rather strange silence. Then we went outside. On the porch, skis and boots lay all in a row near the old couch. A heavy spring rain was falling and we laughed: skis, boots, and this torrential downpour, it was really funny. Serge even said:

"That devil, Julien, he's always out of season!"

Then we put on our anoraks and walked down towards the dam. I had spoken so much about our little beach to Donald that he wanted to see it without any further ado. We slid our way down the slope where the snow had almost completely melted away. I don't know why, but as I grabbed on to the trees so as not to take a header, I was thinking: "We shouldn't! Not today! We should wait a bit longer!" Of all the intuitions I had had these last months, of the strength of my desire to return to Grand Remous, nothing more remained. I was tired and absolutely spiritless. Charles looked at me from time to time and I thought that he too seemed troubled and sad. Serge kept mumbling away that only an American adventurer would drag us into such an escapade. I was quite conscious of this, however: it's always someone coming from somewhere else who opens our eyes. Donald was walking above the sluice gates and we watched him closely, just as children at a circus, sitting there all tense and motionless, observe a tightrope walker on his rope.

"Can I dive in?"

We told him that he was crazy, that the ice had scarcely begun to break up and that he would freeze to death in the dam's whirling waters! He looked at us laughing away and already dipping a leg into the icy current. A little higher up, the ice flows could still be seen trapped against the main gate. Donald let out a funny sort of cry, a sort of Tarzan yelp and vanished into the dark water. For some time, all three of us kept exchanging glances, not daring to say a word. A heavy wind began to rise, blowing our hair about. To me, the beach and the dam had never appeared more sinister. Serge said after a while:

"You really choose suicidal types for boy friends!"

141

I didn't answer. I felt I was going to freeze on the spot and turn into a statue of ice for the rest of eternity. Some strange voice deep down inside me kept saying: "It'll be over soon, you'll see!" I was unconsciously afraid and I didn't want to know what would happen. And then, Donald came back up to the surface. He didn't say a thing, but I understood from his expression and the strange movements he was making to warm himself up again above the sluice gate, that he was about to say something, something he didn't want to say but that he had to, something that would change everything for us. And this is what he said:

"There's a car down there! A rusted pale blue Chevrolet!" [1]

Serge uttered a tiny bird-like cry. Charles and I stood there, gazing at the current, not giving the slightest stir. It was then I saw Julien. He was at the door of giant Trinité Lauzon's old cabin. A woman was standing close by with a baby wrapped in swaddling clothes in her arms. I began running uphill through the trees with frozen mud up to mid-calf. The others were following me, I could hear their breaths at my back. When I finally reached him, I took him in my arms. He was crying and saying over and over:

"You didn't find my stones... you didn't find my stones...."

The young woman went on rocking the baby as she looked at us. I have never seen so much love in a person's gaze, so much tenderness in a human face. The others finally joined us and the woman asked us into the cabin. There was only one large bed and, hanging on the wall, Julien's drawings: trees and faces that we recognized right away. We sat on the ground. The woman made coffee and Julien began talking. His face was more handsome than it had been, but his voice was the same. He said he had followed them on that particular night, what he called "the night at the dam." A storm was rumbling above the hill. The Chevrolet had stopped just at the top of the little cliff. In the lightning's pale glow, he could see their faces and, above all, he could hear them.

"It's tonight or never! Do you understand? I can't take it any more! You've locked me away in that big gloomy house and forced me to make children for you..."

"Forced you ?"

"Yes, forced me, forced me!!!"

Her words rose above the storm, above the roar of the dam and the falls. She shouted:

---

[1]

* *These italicized words spoken by Donald are in English in the original French text.*

"I want to get away and see the world!"

"We can't do that ! The children..."

"You're a weak spineless coward! I should have known. Everything's arranged, you can't back out now ? "

"My love..."

"Oh, don't start that! If I were your love, you'd do what I ask. You coward, you coward!"

There was a flash of lightning. Carmen screamed, climbed out of the car and stepped over to the cliff's edge. Beneath the rain and the glimmering sky, she was as magnificent as terror itself!

"If you won't come, I'll jump! "

"Wait! "

He too got out of the car. There was another flash and the woman dangled her left leg in empty space. As Georges moved towards her, the uproar from the dam muffled his voice. But he must have said what she wanted to hear since Carmen reached out and, in her subdued beauty, allowed herself to be led back to the car through the downpour, her head on his shoulder.

They got back into the Chevrolet and remained there for a while, quietly clutching each other. Georges wept as Carmen kissed his wet hair, saying over and over:

"My love, my love, you're splendid! "

A tremendous clap of thunder split the sky, causing the pines to sway and the dam to quiver. He slipped up to the car from the rear. He had to do it! He couldn't let them leave like that! One good shove with his shoulder and the Chevrolet would tumble down into the sluice gates' whirling waters. His strength was extraordinary! The car spun about for scarcely a minute before it sank. Then he ran back to the mansion. We lay there sleeping like angels. We were alone, we were free!...

It was the woman, Irene, who made him stop by putting the baby, his baby, in his arms. We said nothing. Charles got up and walked to the door: outside a thick curtain of rain was still falling. It was he who said :

"This time, Julien, we won't let them take you away!"

Serge was weeping as he kissed the baby. In the distance, we could hear the dam's swirling waters.

Sainte-Cécile de Milton, August, 1990